THE TURTLE AND THE ROCK

A FUC ACADEMY STORY

AMANDA KIMBERLEY

For my husband,

Thank you for always being my rock.

Always and forever,
Amanda

ACKNOWLEDGMENTS

As always, I'd like to thank Eve, Jess, and Devin for being rock stars in this business. You make writing fun!

Amanda

1

───────

"What the..." Treasure's voice trailed for a moment as she shot up in her bed, startled by her blaring alarm. "Damn it! So soon? I swear I just fell asleep!"

She raked her hands across her face, groaning and continuing to talk to herself—a habit she'd developed since living alone in Harriet's old condo. "Why exactly did Stan want to wait so long to discuss security with me? And why at WANC first thing in the morning?"

The Working and Administration Networking Core—WANC—served as the main academy building for the Furry United Coalition Newbie Academy—FUCN'A. Treasure had finished her cadet training there, and was nearly done with her first understudy apprenticeship to become a certified agent.

Treasure sighed. "Tomorrow, I'm on the plane back to Milos Island. I have to remember how great it will be to see Lear and Harriet. Oh! I need to send my SHIT speech to Harriet for her critique... once I write it. Right. I need to write that speech. Crap!"

The Shifter Hellenic Island Talks—SHIT—was an important event. This year her home island was hosting it, which meant she'd not only be there as a FUC representative but she was also expected to give a speech as the princess and heir. A speech that would live up to her father's standards.

If she forgot the stress of the speech, she was excited to be back around her family. She needed the time around others. She'd grown up with many clutch sisters on Milos Island, and now living without even a roommate left her to live in deafening silence. The conversations with herself were the closest she got to socializing lately, and it was only slightly better than clicking on the TV or streaming satellite radio. When she'd first moved into Harriet's old condo, she'd left the radio or television on all day and night to have the comforting sound of someone else's voice, but after a while, even that seemed as empty as the silence.

Not that Treasure didn't appreciate the living space. When Harriet left for Skyros to marry Treasure's cousin, Lear, she was happy to sublet her condo. But Treasure was learning that she didn't exactly enjoy the lonely apartment life. At least Treasure had only one semester left of her apprenticeship. In just a few more months, she'd be leaving Canada to permanently head back home, where there was always at least one of her siblings willing to talk her ear off about nothing in particular.

Perhaps she was feeling especially lonely because FUCN'A was between sessions and most of the other cadets had already left for break. Plus, many of the FUC agents had already headed to Milos to prep the security for the talks. She would have left earlier too, but her father insisted she wait until he could send the private jet for her.

She rolled out of bed and onto her feet, shrugging on her bathrobe. As she shuffled to the end of the bed, she let out an exaggerated yawn and enjoyed a pronounced stretch before padding to the large master bathroom attached to the bedroom.

She turned on the shower and sighed. The loneliness she experienced might make her uncomfortable, but that didn't mean she was in a hurry to see her father.

The king of Milos Island, a man who stood a towering six-foot-six to her five-foot-five stature, had a presence that could instantly make her feel like she was still a little child.

And that was only his physical presence.

Her father was impossibly difficult to please. The man exuded perfection and always expected it from her as well. She'd work hard on earning an A- on a test, and he'd want to know why she didn't receive an A+.

Treasure understood that her father demanded excellence from her because he took his role as the king of Milos seriously and wanted her to approach her future leadership the same way. The lives of everyone on Milos Island were in their hands, and his sense of duty to them proved second to none.

That all added up to him casting a huge shadow that was nearly impossible for Treasure to face living up to. The man was simply a god to her—and to the inhabitants on Milos Island—and she found it hard to fathom how she'd follow in his footsteps once it was her turn to rule over Milos.

Treasure finished her shower and went to her walk-in closet. The sight of all of her clothes reminded her of the fact that she hadn't packed anything for her trip home yet.

A usual problem for her. She hated packing. And now that she had a meeting with Stan, she'd be even more crunched for time. Good thing it was just a short trip and she wouldn't need more than one carry-on bag's worth of clothes and toiletries.

She shrugged on a tee and a pair of jeans then slipped on her sneakers and called a FUCN'A driver to pick her up and take her to WANC.

***

"So, boss, what's going on that needed me to wake up before the sun?" Treasure asked as she walked into Stan's office.

"Treasure!" Stan greeted her, sitting back in his chair and indicating she take a seat across from him. "Thanks for coming in. Turns out, we have an important dignitary coming in to go over some of the security for the talks."

Treasure squinted at him, confused. "Why would he be coming here? The talks are in a few days. He could just go over security on Milos."

Stan sighed. "I don't know, Treasure. I didn't think to ask my higher-ups why they wanted to indulge the whims of some important prince—no, king. He's a king—King Matco Abara. Would you like me to get on the phone and see if I can get ahold of Alyce, or maybe Miranda or Chase or Viktor, and ask them why King Abara couldn't just have his questions answered when he flies to Milos?"

Treasure stopped herself from rolling her eyes at her boss' dramatic suggestion. "Fine. So we'll all go over the security plans together when he gets here?"

"Exactly," Stan replied. "He works with Bonafide Security, so he's going to be on the team."

"Like me."

"Right." Stan stood from his chair, signaling their talk was over. "He won't be here until noon, so until then, while I have some meetings, I need you to man the desk—take care of any stray students or staff who might come in. Tasha has a day off. Otherwise, I wouldn't have to ask you."

"That's fine," Treasure said, used to the fact that an apprenticeship didn't always mean getting to shadow agents on secret missions. Sometimes it meant admin work and desk-job roles.

But it was okay. The day would be slow, and there likely wouldn't be many people wandering in. Had she been able to stay home that morning, she could have spent the time packing for her trip, but she could also use time at the desk to work on her speech.

"I'm going to try to be back by then, but if I get stuck in my meetings, I just need you to get him started on the paperwork." Standard stuff that all FUCN'A visitors had to complete.

"Sounds great."

As soon as Stan was out of the office, she parked herself at the front desk, pulling one of her many books on Milos out of her bag. "Might as well see if flipping through this sparks an idea or two for my SHIT speech."

2

Mateo Abara, the King Cock of the Madagascar rock agama lizard territories, wasn't used to crowded airports. Or crowds at all, for that matter.

At home, he remained mostly secluded, with just a couple of males and, at most, seven females to deal with at a time. The number of strangers around him at the Vancouver International Airport set him on edge.

If he could have, he would have preferred to land directly at FUCN'A, but the Canadian shifter institution insisted on a certain level of secrecy that wouldn't allow for it. They were set up deep in the mountains, and one needed to transfer to a helicopter or Cessna—something smaller than the international jet—if they wanted to fly in there.

It's not that he hated people—or shifters—he just didn't care for the light-headedness that sometimes followed the experience of being around too many at once. He struggled to keep his sense of reason from being overpowered in those situations. He certainly liked to avoid the occasions when his mind went blank on what to say when faced with an expectant group of people.

He'd been getting better about it since his father had retired from the throne and handed it off to him. It meant taking on all the responsibility of governing as well as inspiring his people with eloquent speeches given before large crowds.

Such as those given at the Shifter Hellenic Island Talks.

He inwardly cringed, remembering that the next SHIT was fast approaching. At least they'd never be as bad as his first. That time, he'd had sweaty palms on the plane, his head spinning after reading and re-reading his notecards, and he could hardly bear the thought of what might happen if he dropped those cards on the way to the podium for his speech.

And then his father had knocked the cards from his hand and told him to talk from the heart. Mateo had been mortified. His father had a natural talent to think on his feet, but until that moment, Mateo hadn't known that he had the ability inside him, too. Sure, it didn't come to him as naturally as it did for his father—Mateo had to fight for every word and thought—but at least he could manage it when needed.

By his third SHIT, he was a pro, all thanks to his father's tough life lesson. He learned that enough prep ahead of time was all he needed to make sure he could speak confidently and answer all follow-up questions. That year's SHIT had been the first time in his life when he came alive and saw that people were understanding and connecting with him.

Now that he was the leader of the red-headed rock agamas, the pressure was even greater.

Especially now that the poaching in Madagascar had been steadily increasing in recent years. So many shifters were going missing, and standing before a crowd and spouting pretty words wasn't enough. He had to *do* something.

That was why he'd started taking an active role as a leader of his regional Bonafide Security contingent.

A leader had to be more than one who gave inspirational speeches. They had to be aware of their surroundings—of potential dangers—and be able to protect themselves and their people when needed.

So it made sense when his father suggested—strongly suggested—he take a trip to FUCN'A before the talks. The academy trained agents for the Furry United Coalition—home of famed croc agent Viktor Smith, a legend in the lizard community. Mateo knew Viktor wouldn't actually be there—as he'd only be there a day and was only scheduled to meet Stan—but it would still be cool to visit and useful to discuss FUC's plans to work security with BS for SHIT.

Mateo signed off on his rental paperwork and found his motorcycle—complete with two helmets. He started her up, listening to the Harley purr like a kitten before he drove off in the direction of FUCN'A.

Half in a daze from jetlag, Mateo found the main administration office of WANC, where he encountered a beautiful blonde with gorgeous green eyes and porcelain skin.

The woman only briefly looked up before informing him, "I need your COC."

Mateo furrowed his brows. Had he misheard her? He cleared his throat. "Um, that's right, I'm the

Cock," he replied, referring to the official term his people used to refer to the leader of the rock agama lizards.

"Funny. However, no COC, no service."

He grew puzzled as to why this woman would address him in such a casual manner. Normally, the Cock was greeted in Madagascar with a loud announcement and trumpets. While he didn't expect that here, he thought it odd that she barely looked up from the manual she busied herself with.

When he didn't reply, the woman finally moved her head toward him slightly, her blonde hair falling around her shoulders. Mateo caught a whiff of her floral perfume, a scent so pleasant that it awakened something in him he'd forgotten about.

"COC—Complaints on Campus form," the woman said when he failed to answer. She slapped a piece of paper on the counter in front of her. "Fill it out, turn it in, and I can start working on your request."

While she spoke, he finally locked on to her beautiful eyes, which struck a verdant hue as they locked onto his. He'd never seen a shade so rich, so pure, or so alive before. Her face was round, and she wasn't slender but had gorgeous curves in all the right places.

He pushed the paper back toward her. "I don't believe you need my COC. Stan is expecting me. I'm King Cock, Mateo Abara—"

"Oh my God." The woman cut him off, lifting a hand to her mouth to cover her look of mortification. "I'm. So. Sorry! Crap, crap, crap!"

The woman ripped the form off the counter and stood, looking in all directions as though she were trying to collect herself or find someone to help her.

"Is Stan in?" Mateo asked, hoping that he could head to the man's office and leave the woman—alluring as he found her—to recover.

"No, he's not!" She looked back at him. "He's in meetings, and he left me here to greet you, and I totally botched it because I got so wrapped up in preparation for this SHIT speech I have to give—that's the Shifter Hellenic Island Talks—"

He cut her off. "I know what SHIT is. I'm preparing for them myself."

"Oh." She finally seemed to slow down and breathe. "You are?"

"I am," he replied. "And I understand the pressure of preparing for them. You said you're giving a speech there?"

She bobbed her cute blonde head and held up her book. "I am, on behalf of Milos Island. I'm Troa sure Garner." She seemed to remember the importance of an introduction and offered him her hand.

Treasure. He caught his breath at the name. "You most certainly are," he said under his breath as he took her hand in his. *A treasure indeed!*

"I'm sorry?"

"Oh! Nothing. Yes, I'm King Mateo of Madagascar. But call me Teo—everyone does," he said with a smile.

It was a lie. No one called him Teo. His people addressed him as King Cock or Your Highness—the exception being his father, who always called him by his full name. Yet, he'd always dreamed that someone special might address him by the shortened version of his name as a term of endearment. Though as time had marched on, he'd grown unsure if he'd ever find anyone who would grace him with such an honor.

"Okay, Teo it is, then." His name sounded so eloquent as it rolled off of her tongue. It was all he had ever hoped for, and it elated him to hear it.

Treasure motioned for him to follow her past the front counter and to a room with a long table. He couldn't help but notice her long and muscular legs, though he was shocked that his mind instantly imagined them wrapped around him.

Such impure thoughts of a woman he hardly knew!

Focus on work. It was important for him to remember that. As his father had always taught him, work before pleasure. Kings had a responsibility to their people first and foremost.

But isn't finding a queen also part of duty? He pushed that thought aside, tuning back into the melodious sound of Treasure's voice.

"We just have some forms for you to fill out—not COC ones!" She laughed, a sound that ticked from his ears to his belly.

"That sounds easy enough," he said, sitting down in front of the papers she indicated.

She sat next to him, awkwardly tapping the table while he wrote until it seemed she couldn't deal with the silence any longer. "So, you're here to discuss security before the talks?"

"I am. And you? How are you working here at FUCN'A but also giving a speech for SHIT?"

"Oh well, you know. I came to FUCN'A to gain some skills so I could defend myself and fight for my people."

"Really?" That was interesting. Treasure was a woman who wasn't just beautiful but was proactive, strong, brave...

"Yep." She sighed as though reluctant to admit the next part. "And I'm giving a speech there, well, because I'm princess and heir to Milos Island."

Mateo glanced up from his paperwork and smiled at her, easily able to appreciate the urge not to brag about a royal status. He liked that she wasn't arrogant. "Well, that explains it."

She nodded. "Yeah."

He saw her mind drift off, and he searched for a new topic, eager to keep her engaged. "So, how's the weather here? I have to admit I was leery about how cold it might be, even now in the springtime. My phoenix side did *not* want to encounter any snow."

"Luckily, Vancouver isn't the worst. Some of the other cadets tell me horror stories about *Winterpeg* over in Manitoba, but in BC, the weather is pretty mild, and springtime is usually very pretty."

"Winterpeg?" He laughed, imagining a Santa's workshop-type city, before going back to the forms in front of him.

It grew quiet again, but it seemed Treasure couldn't handle silence for very long, as she soon asked, "So you're attending the talks, too?"

He smiled, enjoying her chatty nature. "I am. In fact, as long as I receive Stan's approval, I'm hoping to gain authorization to help out with some aerial surveillance during the event."

"Oh, awesome! I'm hoping Stan will let me work with BS in guarding the dignitaries, too!"

"But you're also preparing a speech and acting as host since it's on your island?"

Her face darkened at that. "Yeah. With SHIT in Milos this year, my father wants me to make a presentation, but it's my first one. I haven't really done much in that kind of official capacity except wave and smile at our people until now."

"You'd rather work security, though." Just like him.

"Yeah, I'm more comfortable in that area, and I know I'm going to be distracted with the Zagan stuff anyway, so I'll be happier working with BS and not being sidelined."

"Zagan." Mateo basically spat the name. "The guy going after royal blood."

"That's the one," Treasure chewed on her lower lip, drawing Mateo's attention to their plump, rosy softness. "We never had to worry about shifters being kidnapped and experimented on in Greece ever before—one of the perks of living on an island, I guess. But now? Everything has changed. Leatherback shifters we thought lost to fishermen's nets were discovered in labs, so now we know we're no longer safe."

"That's rough." Mateo resisted the temptation to take her hand in his and offer her reassurance. "Madagascar has seen its fair share of abductions as well, specifically with our lemur shifters. Sitting back and letting others take care of security is no longer an option. It's part of why I had to be with the BS teams, protecting my people."

"Zagan's an experiment," Treasure stated, scowling. "An unnatural abomination, looking to do the same thing that happened to him to other shifters."

"I'm also an experiment," he informed her, not wanting Zagan to be the sole representative of his hybrid kind. "Red-headed rock agama lizard crossed with a phoenix. We're not all bad, you know."

She gasped. "I'm so sorry! I shouldn't have said that!"

"It's okay. You didn't know."

"You mentioned lizards, and you mentioned your phoenix, but I just didn't click all that together in my mind. Besides, I shouldn't have said such a broad statement that suggested I felt that way about all experiments. I don't think that, I swear! We have lots of experiments being rehabilitated here, and they're all innocent, good shifters!"

"Treasure, it's okay." He tried to calm her.

She took a breath, and then her thoughts seemed to move to a new topic. "I bet you're gorgeous when you shift."

"Only when shifted?" he teased.

"I'm sorry. I mean, it's not that you aren't gorgeous now!" Treasure's eyes widened, and her cheeks radiated a bright red heat.

"It's okay. I understand." This time, he couldn't stop himself from placing his hand over hers.

The moment he did, a current of heat radiated from her body, electrifying his. A sense of desire enveloped him as his manhood strained at the zipper of his black jeans.

To him, there was no doubt that Treasure Garner, princess of Milos Island, was his mate. His body had never sung for anyone else like that before.

"No, it's not okay. I should be a little more professional. I mean, sure, normally, I don't have a filter with anyone. But it's not the best quality, because it's always getting me into trouble. I'm a princess, after all, and really, I should refrain from saying things like that—especially with you. That was inappropriate. It wasn't proper for a princess to say, and it most certainly wasn't becoming of a FUC field agent."

"But, Treasure—"

She stood, cutting him off. "I'm going to leave you to this paperwork while I go die a little from embarrassment over at my desk."

He tried to protest, but she was out of the room before he could tell her that the attraction she was feeling was mutual.

3

Treasure practically ran back to the front desk, only stopping to pour herself a cup of cold water from the office dispenser to cool down.

God, what I wouldn't give for a cold shower right now!

Teo the King Cock was *drop-dead* gorgeous. Her inner diva protested leaving his side, but Treasure couldn't stay in the same room with him for another second. Her thoughts had been flooded with ideas of pawing at his perfect posterior and nibbling at all parts of his magnificently muscled body.

If she had any intention of keeping things professional with him, she had to step away and cool down pronto.

She finished her water and caught her breath

when Stan came barreling into the office area. He caught sight of her and barked in a low, guttural growl, "Where is the dignitary? You were supposed to stick by his side!"

"He's filling out paperwork in the conference room. I stepped out to get some water. I am still allowed to hydrate, aren't I?"

"Of course, but—"

"I mean, I'm a turtle, remember?" Treasure dramatically pointed a finger at herself, enjoying seeing her boss a bit flustered. She played it up, mostly because it pulled her attention away from her wicked thoughts about their guest. "Water is *very* important for my well-being."

"Yes, well, I, uh..." Stan cleared his throat. "Did you start going over security stuff yet?"

"No, we've only made it to the paperwork."

"All right." Stan cleared his throat again. "Sorry I snapped, but I was concerned when I saw you here without him."

She crossed her arms and made a clucking sound while shaking her head. "Did you take your nap yet, Stan? Sometimes you are such a grump!"

"I'm not kidding, Treasure! He's a dignitary! He shouldn't be alone—even for a second!"

Alone time is exactly what I want with that man— lots and lots of alone time.

Treasure, pull yourself together, woman!

"Is it my imagination, or does everyone around here forget that I'm a dignitary too? An important princess, heir to an island, future ruler, that kind of thing..."

Stan blinked his eyes twice before attempting a response. "I—"

"You know, Stan, this may come as a shock to you, but we royals are quite capable of doing things on our own. In fact, I'm pretty sure I can conquer all the SHIT and be my own BS, for FUC's sake!"

"Treasure, no one said that you can't handle being part of the Bonafide Security at the Shifter Hellenic Island Talks. Obviously, we wouldn't have authorized you and his highness back there to be part of the security team if we didn't think you could handle it. You'll both blend in because you and your people are regulars there. I just want the two of you to get to know each other well so you'll be in lock-step during the talks."

I agree. I think the better we know each other, the better a team we'll be. I should take him back to my place and get the ball rolling on that...

Treasure shook her head and let out a breath,

more exasperated with the non-stop dirty thoughts going through her head than anything her boss said. She had to find a way to put her feelings aside so she could be in the same room with the gorgeous god.

Though that idea alone made her inner diva do cartwheels. *Being so close to his body...*

Everything about him made her body sing a symphony of sensations. Sensations she figured she would never have again. It had been nearly a decade since she'd even been on a date—let alone been attracted to anyone. She'd ignored all desires to date, focusing instead on her political studies so her father would take her seriously. She wanted to make her people proud of her leadership, and that meant that love wasn't in the cards for her.

Teo...

Oh, good lord! I am doing it again!

There's got to be a way for me to put my feelings aside and work with him. I just have to find a way to push on. Besides... how much of a pull could this sex god really have on me, anyway? I mean, we just met!

She let out a long breath.

Silly girl! He has plenty already with you, and this can only mean one thing...

He's my mate.

Shit!

As they entered the room, Mateo stood up to greet them. Treasure crossed her arms over her chest. Her heart pounded so hard she worried Stan and Mateo might see it trying to jump out of her chest.

"Stan! It's a pleasure to meet you in person, finally."

"The pleasure is all mine," Stan said as he grasped Mateo's extended hand and gave it a firm shake. "I know the two of you had a chance to meet. Have you had a chance to complete the paperwork?"

"I have. I've got your TURDS right here," Mateo replied, sliding Stan the completed Truthful and Unfettered Reconciliation to Defend our Secrets form—the FUC equivalent to a non-disclosure agreement.

"Perfect, so now we can focus on the talk's security."

Stan handed Teo a tablet, and Treasure pulled out her own for him to send the encrypted file to. For the rest of the afternoon, they went over the plan, which included basics like which agents would be assigned to each island or territory and keeping dignitaries a certain distance away from the crowd.

"In the past, we never had a barrier, but given the seriousness of this whole Zagan thing, we may want to consider this as an option," Treasure said. "My father and many of his advisors, as well as my younger sisters, will be up on the stage listening to the others talk. I'll have a vantage point to see them before anyone tries to make a move, but the barrier would help to deter anyone from rushing the stage."

"A barrier around the stage area, at the very least," Teo agreed.

They continued on, going over the layout of the island and the conference facility and where both BS and FUC would be stationed.

Treasure completely lost track of time—and luckily, also managed to put away all her dirty thoughts during the planning time—until a gurgling noise had both her and Mateo looking at Stan.

"Guess we've been here a while," Stan said, turning a bit red while he rubbed his belly.

"I'm a bit hungry myself," Mateo admitted. "We've covered most of it, I think. Perhaps we could head somewhere for food and see if there are any last details we've left off?"

"The Hub, in town, has great food," Stan offered, already standing and leading the way to the exit. "Not that the cafeteria here isn't great too, but The Hub has darts and pool if you want to unwind a bit."

"But, I, well—" Treasure tried to protest, but Teo

had already followed Stan out of the room. As she crossed the threshold, she felt a surge of energy flow through her body as Teo brushed her shoulder with his.

"He's right, Treasure. Let's continue this over a nice meal."

The heat that was radiating from his body was intoxicating, and she searched for any reason to escape. She had to have a chance to sober up from her desire of wanting to rock his world. "Teo, I haven't even packed yet. I need to go back to the condo and do that before I think of anything else."

She split from the group, grabbing her things from behind the counter and making a beeline toward the exit. The electricity between them was so intense that her body ached from moving away from him. She had no idea how she'd maintain a working relationship with that man. But she had to come up with one quickly so she could concentrate on keeping everyone safe at the talks.

It could prove disastrous if she found it this diffi-cult to separate her sheer attraction to him from her duties.

Damn it, Stan! Why did you have to pair me up with a sex god?

She almost had a foot out of WANC's front door

when Teo caught up to her, stopping her with a gentle touch on her elbow. "Hey, I understand if you're in a time crunch, but maybe I can go with you? We could order food in and make sure we've gone over every last detail while you pack?"

Treasure let out a sigh. She'd almost made it to the home stretch. That cold shower she'd needed had been within reach.

But her inner diva danced with glee, knowing she now couldn't escape the gorgeous god. She almost smelled the scent of strawberries dripping from his light reddish-blond hair.

He is just so delicious.

But, girl, you have a job to focus on...

His eyes appeared to be as blue as the Aegean Sea. Such deep, stunning pools that gave her a sense of serenity she yearned to bask in.

God, I could get lost in those eyes all day. And I wish he'd press that rock-hard chest against mine.

I wonder how big he is, though...

He's got to be great if he's part phoenix.

He must be pure flames in bed.

Stop it, Treasure! Just stop it!

"Earth to Treasure?"

Treasure's eyes widened as Teo wave a hand in

front of her. "I'm sorry. I must have blanked for a minute. Just going over the itinerary in my head."

"Is it okay if I accompany you back to your place so we can talk while you're packing?"

"Oh yeah, packing," she said with a frown. "That's fine. It shouldn't take me too long to pack my *oh-shit* bag."

Teo's brows narrowed. "You named a duffel bag after the Shifter Hellenic Island Talks?"

"Oh! No! I meant a slang term for stuffing your bag because you forgot you have to be somewhere," she said with a chuckle.

"I never will get used to these strange acronyms."

"Me neither."

"Treasure," Stan called up, finally reaching them. "I did mention that you're to stick by King Mateo's side tonight, right? You're the agent assigned to his security."

Treasure blinked in surprise. *Of course* Stan would add that on to everything else.

She could insist that Stan do it himself, but when Teo's eyes drifted to her again, she knew that she was the only one he needed. "I've got him covered," she said.

"That works for me," Teo replied.

"Fantastic. And you're flying together back to

Milos tomorrow morning, with your royal security. The FUC agents already on the island will be ready for your arrival."

"Oh?" Treasure looked at Teo quizzically.

"You didn't know we'd be flying together? It just made sense not to have to separate private international jets going to the same place at the same time."

"I didn't know that, but if it's been cleared by everyone, it's fine by me. Way better to fly with friends than have a whole plane alone." Treasure gave him a bright smile, trying to hide the fact that she found it extremely difficult to stop thinking about this guy sexually for five whole minutes, and she had zero clues on how she'd get through a whole flight being so close to him.

"All right, great. Have a good night and a great time at the talks." Stan didn't bother waiting for them as he hurried to his car.

They were alone again. "So, you sure you want to go back to your apartment first? Because I could really go for some food."

Treasure sighed. Every last chance of running from Teo had been taken from her. She might as well accept her fate.

"All right, let's head to the Hub."

4

———

There was no denying she was attracted to Teo, but now she needed to be his personal bodyguard, too. Any ideas of having any kind of tryst with the man halted with Stan's news. Treasure had even more reason to suppress her feelings and focus on his safety. One hesitation on her part could mean death for them both.

"I don't have a car here. I usually get one of the FUCN'A cars to drive me," she explained as she pulled out her phone.

"No need," he said, placing his hand on her phone to stop her from dialing. "I have a rental."

She saw he pointed to a cherry-red motorcycle sitting in a visitors' parking space. "Oh."

Teo knit his brows. "Is there something wrong with my mode of transportation?"

"No. No! It's a very nice bike."

"But?"

"I've never been on a motorcycle before. I'm not sure what to do."

"I'll teach you. And don't worry, I have a helmet for you. I ordered two because I knew Stan was going to give me an agent, so I wanted to be sure I had them covered. Literally."

She let out a nervous laugh. "Okay, that's good. I'm just a little worried. That's all."

"As long as you don't mind being so close to me, you'll be fine."

If only he knew how very much she wanted to be extremely close to him...

She used her feeling of desire toward Teo to find the courage to approach his steel beast.

She stood still while he placed a helmet on her head, and she lifted her chin so he could adjust the strap to fit her. She even took the hand he offered as she swung a leg over and settled on the back seat.

All while trying not to shake with combined excitement and nerves.

Teo's eyes glinted at her while he strapped on his helmet. She held her breath when he slid on the bike in front of her, her heart pounding hard—both from the trepidation of the ride and proximity to her hot rock.

She drank in his musky scent. A combination of vetiver, patchouli, and cedarwood hit her first. She then caught traces of sweet citrus, musk, and moss in the mix. It was a pleasant tease to her nose, and she couldn't help taking several deep breaths to commit the cologne to memory.

He turned his head, speaking. "Hold on to my belt or wrap your arms around me, whichever you're more comfortable with."

"Okay," she replied, reaching for his belt.

"Then, while we're riding, just make sure to lean the same way I do. Understand?"

"Yes." Treasure swallowed hard.

"Well then, let's blow this Popsicle stand. Ready?"

"Let's do it!" She put as much enthusiasm into her voice as she could.

He fired up the bike, making it roar and vibrate below them.

She stifled a gasp, tightening her grip on his belt as Teo guided the motorcycle through the parking lot and then onto the only road that led to or from the Academy.

As he picked up speed, she leaned into him, taking him up on the offer to wrap her arms around him, feeling safer pressed into his back than she did sitting back against the bar behind her seat.

The breeze tickled her body, and she immediately realized why the phoenix shifter would like such a ride. The rush of the wind could be likened to flying—or so she could only imagine, and that made her wonder even more what he looked like when he shifted.

It must be a glorious transformation, much like the rock-hard body of his human half. Her inner turtle gave a high-pitched squeal at the mere thought of him clad in all of his human glory.

The ride was short—much too short. It seemed they'd just started riding when he was already pulling into the Hub.

A pang of emptiness hit her when he turned off the bike. When he dismounted, only the warmth from his backside lingered around her thighs, and the rest of her body shivered from his absence.

He placed his helmet down and then helped her off the bike.

"My hair must look silly," she said as she removed the helmet, handed it to Teo, and fumbled to smooth down her static ends.

To her surprise, he cupped her cheek, turning her face to look into her eyes. "You look adorable."

The heat instantly rose again, and she reminded herself of the necessity to quash it so she could focus on her protection duty.

She stepped back from him and gestured with her head toward the bike. "You seem really comfortable on that thing. I'm guessing you ride at home?"

"Sure do," he replied, shoving his hands into his pockets after placing the helmets on the bike. "It's the phoenix in me. I can't resist the wind in my face, and the only way to accomplish that same exhilarating experience on the ground is by riding."

She nodded. "Yeah, that's what I'd figured. It's kind of like me with the sea. There's nothing like it. And sometimes, when I miss home, the closest I can get is taking a bath or shower. There're no beaches near here. A waterfall, a small lake, but no salty sea."

"Then I bet you're more than excited to be setting foot back home soon."

She nodded then gestured to the pub. "Shall we go in?"

5

———

They walked in and found the place crowded. "I didn't know this tiny mountain town *had* so many people," Teo commented, speaking loud enough to be heard over the televisions blaring sports channels.

"Well, they all gather here, that's for sure," Treasure replied.

He gestured to the bar. "Looks like there are two spots there if that's okay with you."

"Sounds fine."

As soon as they sat, the bartender walked over, placing napkins down in front of each of them. "What can I get you?"

"We'll take a menu. No drinks for me. I'm on duty," Treasure answered.

"If you're on duty, so am I," Teo added, glad for the excuse to not imbibe. Otherwise, he would have a harder time holding back from her.

He could still feel her arms around him, her legs squeezing him tight as they rode from the Academy. He'd never had such a good ride in his entire life—all seven minutes of it.

Seven minutes of heaven.

The bartender handed them menus and placed two glasses of water on the bar.

Teo watched Treasure while she read her menu, looking as comfortable as could be in the little hole-in-the-wall pub. He'd learned enough about her in their short time together to see that she wasn't what he would have expected from a princess. She wasn't like any of the ones he'd dated in the past, who cared only about their own status and power.

Treasure cared about her people, her duty. She wanted to be the best ruler she could, to make her father proud, and to serve her country.

She was the one—his mate.

The woman he was going to marry.

But she really had no idea who he was.

When the beautiful blonde in the WANC office revealed she was the princess and heir of Milos, Teo realized exactly why his father had sent him on a last-minute trip to FUCN'A.

And why King Ambrose of Milos had suggested Teo take his private jet.

He should have said something right there, but shouldn't she have known? She knew she was betrothed, right? She knew the alliance was between her country and his, right?

So as long as she didn't address it, he didn't. What was he supposed to say?

Our fathers have been conspiring for years to make us meet, but even after I finally agreed, you still refused, and now they've tricked us, and it turns out I really like you and want this to work...

And then what? She'd turn furious at the trickery, blame him, slam the door in his face, and he'd ruin the chance at uniting their kingdoms *and* lose a woman he was quickly falling for?

His body resonated with hers in a way that was different from that of any other woman he had known before her. No one piqued his interest long enough to last past date two.

But Treasure? He didn't want their first day together to end, ever. That was a stark comparison to anything he had ever known before. He couldn't know if she felt the same, but one truth stood out above the rest.

Treasure can't learn the truth. She's my one and only. I can't lose that. I can't lose her.

When Teo first learned of the contract that was made between the kings, which would force him to marry a stranger, he'd refused to acknowledge it. He spent his young life dating and acting as though he had a choice in who he'd spend his life with.

Each time the kings attempted to arrange a meeting, Teo disappeared.

Little did he know the princess was doing the same.

It was only after he stepped into his role as king that he understood the importance of the alliance—especially with threats like Zagan out there. They needed to unite the kingdoms and ensure the next generation.

But despite Teo's changed position on the betrothal, the princess had still refused every invitation to meet.

He'd been determined that the cold-feet game would come to an end at the talks this year. The princess would have to meet him. She couldn't flee her own island, which meant Teo would finally lay eyes on her. Finally meet her. Finally cement his alliance with King Ambrose.

Apparently, their fathers didn't feel as confident, as they'd clearly arranged to trick them into meeting.

And if Treasure learned he was the prince she was betrothed to, she would never want to see him again. That made his heart cave within his chest.

"Earth to Teo." Treasure brought him back to her, waving a hand in front of him.

"Oh! Sorry." The bartender had returned. As Teo had been preoccupied with his thoughts instead of reading the menu, he picked a random item and hoped for the best.

"Penny for your thoughts," Treasure teased once the bartender left them again.

"I was just trying to remember everything we went over with Stan for the security detail. We should probably talk more strategy before the night escapes us."

"Yeah, we probably should. I liked your idea about aerial surveillance. We've never had that before. Of course, we've never had any FUC agents covering our BS's ass either."

"The Avian Soaring Security works with Milos' BS?" Teo asked with a furrowed brow.

"Oh, they do, but I wasn't referring to ASS. I meant ass, as in our backside," Treasure said with a laugh. "Those damn acronyms!"

"Ah!"

"Hey, since you are part phoenix, wouldn't you be part of Avian Soaring Security too?"

Teo shrugged. "I think eventually I'll link up with ASS, but my father had insisted on visiting FUC today."

"Well, in that case, remind me to thank your father because I'm pleased we got to meet before the talks." She raised her glass of water to him.

"Treasure," he said, lost in her eyes as they clinked glasses, "I have to tell you... I like you a lot, and I get the sense that the feeling is mutual."

He placed his glass down and touched her face, remembering how she'd pulled away from him outside but taking the chance to stroke her porcelain cheek with his thumb anyway.

"Teo, we shouldn't," she said, her lips only a breath away from his.

"Treasure, I really, really like you, and ever since I met you this afternoon, this is all I've wanted." She hadn't pulled back or slapped his hand away, so he did it. He leaned forward, crashing his lips upon hers.

The kiss was hungry, searing with so much warmth it was as if he was back in Madagascar during the middle of summer. He'd kissed plenty of women before her, but this was the first time a kiss gave him a taste of heaven.

But he quickly crashed back down to Earth when she pulled away from him, turning her head just as the bartender returned with two plates.

They both thanked the bartender then dug into their food in silence.

Finally, Treasure spoke. "Teo, there's something I need to tell you, and I'm not quite sure how to put it. I guess it's because what I'm about to say never really mattered to me until I met you. And this isn't easy for me to say because I don't want to hurt you."

"You can tell me anything."

She swallowed hard and took a deep breath before continuing. "I'm not free to date. I'm betrothed. My father promised me to a prince a long, long time ago."

"Oh," Teo replied. *It's now or never. Tell her.*

But he couldn't. He just couldn't risk her turning on him.

"Yes. I've always refused to recognize it. I don't even know who he is or where he's from. As far as I ever considered, I've not agreed to it, it wasn't my choice, and I hate that. I understand arranged marriages of the past, when people didn't leave their homes very often, so it's not like they'd get out and find love, or even… their mates."

"Mate."

"Yes, mate."

"So you feel it too?"

"Yes."

His heart surged. Nothing else mattered except for the fact that his Treasure felt the same about him.

Treasure continued. "Now that I've met you, my mind is made up. I'm going to inform my father that there is absolutely no chance of fulfilling the betrothal."

"Treasure—"

She held up a hand. "No, don't say anything. I mean, unless you think I'm getting too far ahead of things. I'm being presumptuous. I just thought, if we both think we're mates…"

"No, that's not it, at all. I want to be with you. I see a future with you. That much I'm absolutely sure of." He took her hand and tried to land on the right way to reveal things to her. Clearly, she felt guilt over not fulfilling the betrothal, and he could help that.

"But your betrothal, it's part of your duty, and in

everything else you do, you show how dedicated to your people you are. If your father thinks the alliance would help your people, don't you think he might be right?"

Treasure shook her head, her mouth forming a tight frown. "No, I don't. These people have tried my entire life to force me into it, and for that, I don't trust them."

"What?"

"After I refused invitations for so long, they started trying to trick me into meeting the prince. I'm sure they figured if I met him, he could turn on the charm and force little old me to fall in love with him, and then they win."

Teo's blood ran cold. If he revealed himself now, it would be a disaster. She'd accuse him of tricking her...

"My father is friends with my betrothed's father, and he's let that cloud his judgment. No matter what benefits the marriage might bring to Milos, I know there are other options. I just thought you should know this all up front because I really am falling for you, Teo. But for us to have any chance of being together, I have to tell my father about us, and he is just going to have to understand that I want to be with you and not some conniving prince trying to get his hands on more power and territory."

"I agree," he said, realizing it really was their only chance. Once she broke off the betrothal, she'd no longer believe he was trying to trick her into something she didn't want.

So, she doesn't have a clue that I am her betrothed. But if she did, she'd hate me for it. She'd think I tricked her.

It gutted him to lie to her, but now it seemed he had little choice. If she learned the truth, she'd think he had set this whole chance meeting up himself, when, in fact, it was his father that had done so.

6

———

Her condo wasn't far from the Hub. She gave him instructions, and he easily found it, lamenting once again that the ride was too short.

He followed her to her door.

"Make yourself at home. I have wine, or if you'd prefer, some beer in the fridge," she said as she let him inside.

She locked the door behind them, and he watched her fumble with her keys and purse while placing them on the credenza in the entry. He tossed his bag on the floor, not able to handle another second without her in his arms.

She easily accepted his kiss this time, and he drank in her perfume, which held a hint of the sea in its intoxicating aroma.

He wasn't sure how long the kiss had gone on for —a minute, maybe two? And then he realized that they'd walked farther into the condo when they bumped into a chair. Instinctually, he sank into the leather cushion of the oversized tawny brown wingchair and pulled her on top of him. She straddled him, and the friction between their bodies sent waves of pleasure through him. Her hips rubbed on him, and she let out a deep moan of pleasure.

He moved his lips, grazing her cheek before nibbling on her earlobe.

"Teo..." she gasped.

"I love the way you say my name," he growled as his palms glided down her shoulders and greedily took her breasts into his hands.

"Teo." She said it again as his thumbs teased her nipples through the fabric that covered them.

"I want you, Treasure." He slid one hand lower, tracing a line over the junction of her thighs, making her buck at the gesture.

"I want to kiss you here," he said as he teased the lobe of her ear with more kisses. "Can I kiss you here?"

Treasure let out another moan of pleasure before she nodded. His fingers began to fumble with the button of her jeans. He gently tugged at the button and zipper and waited for her to stand so he could glide the jeans and her panties down her legs. His lips followed them as he knelt before her, feathering kisses on her legs before he hovered over her center.

"God, you are beautiful, Treasure," he said as he placed his thumb over her folds and made gentle circles.

Her womanhood was poised for pleasure as his finger plunged into her center. His tongue teased her essence as it slicked over her wet folds. She laced her hands around the back of his thick and wavy hair and bucked with pleasure once more.

"That's it, baby, come for me," he said as he reached his free hand up and worked it underneath her T-shirt and bra. He teased the first one then the other pert nipple as he continued to lap her delicate sweetness.

He felt her knees begin to shake, and he continued to pleasure her with his mouth until she melted before him. He helped her to the floor as she crumpled, spent from the gratification he had given her. He pulled her into his chest.

"I'm so lucky to have a treasure like you," he said as he kissed her cheek. "I think I'm really falling for you, my darling."

Treasure smiled. "I'm falling for you too."

As she lay in his arms, his head raced. He needed to make things right, and the only way he could see that happening was if he could speak to both of their fathers and ensure they'd never mention the truth to her. This seemed to be the only way she'd still be his, and she wouldn't know the difference.

"I'm having a lot of fun, Teo. More than I've had in a long time," she said as she bit her lip. "I hope what I said earlier didn't hurt you."

"No. No! I completely understand how hard a father's will can be. I've got similar problems with mine."

"Good," she said as she leaned up and brushed his lips. "I don't ever want to upset you."

He caressed her hair.

"I never want to hurt you either." His lips crashed onto hers again as he kissed her with renewed hunger at his intent to never allow her to learn the truth.

"God, I want you every chance that I can get," he said as his lips hovered over hers.

"I want you too, Teo," she whispered over his lips.

He kissed her again with urgency as his palms explored each curve of her body and finally freed her of her shirt and bra.

"Which way is your bedroom?"

She pointed, and he scooped her into his arms, carrying her down the hall and through the door then placing her gently on the bed.

As he straddled her, he claimed her lips again, the kiss so searing he hoped she understood she was his. And once she parted her lips for him to enter her delicious mouth, he figured she understood how much he wanted to make her his. He explored every inch of her mouth as he made haste of the buttons and zippers on his clothing, tossing all the fabric to the floor while he focused on the thrill of their skin-to-skin contact.

"You are absolutely perfect," he said in a low growl while tracing the curves of her body with his index finger.

Her body arched and shivered in response as his manhood hovered over her center. She palmed his backside, making him growl with pleasure once more. It was all the encouragement he needed to finally enter her in one smooth motion that earned him a gentle cry. She matched each of his thrusts in perfect unison until they were both spent from a glorious release.

Teo kissed her forehead and then pulled her to his chest.

"I don't know about you, but I could use a long, hot shower," Treasure said with a wry smile as she wrapped her arms around his waist.

"A shower sounds lovely, but I'd much rather spend some time with you in the tub," he replied with a smile.

"Oh, really? Well, I think that can be arranged. I'll get the water running and grab some towels."

"I'll go to the kitchen for the wine you mentioned before."

Teo quickly returned to her with the glasses and already had the bottle of cabernet opened. He poured two glasses as Treasure turned off the faucet from the filled tub. He helped her inside and followed right behind.

"Thank you," she said, accepting the glass of wine he passed to her.

"Treasure, you said you wanted to be upfront with me when you told me you were promised to someone. Well, I, too, need to make a similar admission."

"Teo, it wouldn't surprise me if your father had an arrangement for you to marry someone, as well. I mean, it's commonplace with royals."

"Well, I'm glad it doesn't surprise you, but it bothers me nonetheless. That's why I'm going to be having a talk with my father about you once we land. It's important to me we make our wishes known to both of our families," he said with a smile of contentment for finally coming up with something to say to her about the arranged marriage. He raised his glass in Treasure's general direction. Treasure joined her glass to his until it made a clinking sound.

"That sounds like a perfect idea to me," she said, returning the smile.

He took a sip to try to drown out the words that he was afraid might follow. The lie was killing him, but he couldn't tell her. He was certain he'd lose her for sure. She'd never believe it wasn't all an elaborate maneuver to manipulate her.

And she'd only blame him.

His stomach dropped.

Treasure placed the glass on the ledge of the bath and turned on the jets to the tub. She then laid her head back on a bath pillow and let out a hum of contentment.

"Mmm... this is the life! That's for sure!"

"You sound like you won't ever be able to do something like this once you go back."

"That's because I probably won't," Treasure said with a frown while taking another sip of her wine. "Being a princess isn't easy. And once I'm done with my apprenticeship and return to Milos for good, my father wants me to take on more responsibilities so I'm better prepared to take over the throne once he has retired. I'm really not sure if I can handle all of it."

"It was hard for me too. I always assumed that my father would be there to offer me guidance when it came to ruling the territory, or he'd simply make the decisions himself. It was too hard to imagine that I'd be on my own. I didn't want to let him or our people down."

"That's my problem too. I always feel like I'm a kid all over again and I'm trying to fill his shoes. Shoes that are way too big to step into."

"Treasure, you are a strong and beautiful woman. I don't think you need to follow anyone, because you possess the qualities to be a great leader in your own right. No one expects you to do everything the same as your father."

Treasure nodded. "You know, I never thought about it that way. I guess you are right."

Teo smiled and reached for the loofah that was on the ledge of the tub. "Come here. Let me wash you. It'll get rid of some of that stress that is building up in your shoulders."

"It's that obvious?"

"Yes. Yes, it is. Treasure, the weight of the world doesn't need to be on your shoulders all day and all night. You've got to find a way to put some of that stress aside so you can sleep at night. That's the first lesson I learned when I became the ruler."

"I understand that all too well. Even Father has said the same to me on more than one occasion. But I'm not very good at that. It's so hard for me to wind down."

"Well, I'm here now, and I'm very good at helping with letting go of tension." He squeezed some liquid soap onto the loofah and made tiny circles on each of her shoulders before leaning into her forehead and kissing it gently. "Turn around so I can get your back."

She swished around in the large tub until her back was facing him. He made small circles on her back, paying great attention to her spine between her shoulder blades, until she let out a hum of relaxation. As he massaged each vertebra, she let out several moans of pleasure. When he finished, she leaned back into his chest, and he wrapped his arms around her.

"You have no idea how much I've really needed this. I miss the serenity of the ocean. You just can't replicate the same calming effect as sitting in a pool of sea water. I really miss the beach on Milos."

"The sea must balance you, as the sunsets do for me in Madagascar. There is no other place in the world that has a sunset quite like ours."

"Oh, but I bet Milos can give it a run for its money. The way the sun reflects off of the water is spectacular, and I've seen hints of true red in the sky on Milos. I've also seen lavender mixed in with the reds and blues. But you are right. Madagascar sunsets are quite unique and probably my favorite to view in all the world."

"You've been to Madagascar?" His heart almost stopped.

"Once. My father was trying to trick me into going to meet with that prince I was telling you about. We made a stop-over there, which is when I caught onto what he was doing and refused to move from my seat on the plane until he agreed to tell the pilot to fly home. Apparently, I made things very hard between my father and the prince's father. They were in peace talks for weeks." She let out a sigh. "It was a long time ago. Hopefully long enough that they'll both finally agree to dissolve the agreement."

Teo just nodded. He wasn't sure what else he

could say to her without revealing that he was, in fact, the prince she should have met all those years back.

Was there any way he could convince her that what had happened between them might be for the best? They'd both been so stubborn. Neither had wanted a betrothal. He wondered if it would have ever worked between them in any other way than this.

No. She just can't know the truth. I can't lose her. She's my one true mate.

"Teo, I just hope I can convince my father of our match. I'm not sure how he will take it. I mean, I know I have to be strong. And I can be convincing."

"Why don't we focus on relaxing in the bathtub rather than worrying about what you want to say to your father? We both have a long flight, and we need at least a little sleep before that long plane ride."

"As always, you are right."

They finished bathing and then left the tub. Teo wrapped her in a towel before he dried himself off. She led him back to her bedroom.

"Teo, will you hold me?"

Teo hopped onto the bed and pulled her into the length of his body.

"Always, my love. Always."

7

Treasure woke up in heaven.

Her rock's arms were around her, and she couldn't believe what she'd allowed to happen.

Not only did she allow herself to throw all thoughts of staying professional out the window but she'd also admitted to someone that she was betrothed.

Not for long, she thought, sneaking out of bed. *So help me, I will get Father to see reason.*

She didn't have much time before they needed to leave to make the hour's drive to the airport, and she still hadn't packed. She quickly dressed and then tore apart her closet, tossing in everything she could think she might need—keeping in mind that most of her formalwear was already back home.

As she shoved the last bra into her bag, she heard a knock. She looked up and saw Teo leaning into the frame of the closet door. His white tee clung to him. The thin fabric etched hard, distinct outlines of his pecs. Her heart began to flutter as thoughts of caressing each dip of his defined, chiseled curves flooded her once more.

"Teo, hey."

"You need any help packing?"

"Actually, I just finished."

"Just in time. Are you calling a driver, or are you feeling brave enough to ride the bike with me? I can strap both our bags on it if you're up for it."

"Let's do it."

The sun was just coming up over the horizon as they returned the motorcycle to the rental office and then boarded the private plane. The pilot welcomed them onboard, and the flight attendant took their bags.

"I will have drinks served once we take off. Until then, sit back and relax while we prepare for liftoff," the attendant said as she returned to the crew area.

Treasure sat down on one of the buttery ivory-colored leather lounges. Teo sat on the one opposite her. "I've never seen a princess pack so light before," he said to her with a toothy grin. "Does that mean you aren't a diva?"

"Yeah. I'm mostly not a diva, but that doesn't mean I don't like dressing up for balls and the like."

"Though you likely didn't bring your ball gowns to FUCN'A."

"That's correct." She laughed, imagining herself showing up to a training exercise in anything other than fatigues. "All my fancy stuff is back home."

"How much longer do you have for your training here?" Teo asked.

"I just have this last semester to complete, and then I'm back home."

"You seem conflicted about that."

Treasure sighed, looking out the window as the plane began to move down the runway. "You're not wrong. I miss my family—all my sisters, my cousin Lear and his wife, Harriet, who live on a nearby island—but I'll miss it here. Honestly, I think what I might miss the most is not being under my father's thumb."

"*That* I can relate to. I was never a fan of being under my father's thumb either—especially when I had to make decisions for our territory. I understand my father is older and wiser, but sometimes a new perspective is valuable."

"Oh! Tell me about it! My father insists on old traditions."

"Like betrothals," Teo said softly.

Teo's words about duty had haunted her since he'd said it.

But your betrothal, it's part of your duty, and in everything else you do, you show how dedicated to your people you are. If your father thinks the alliance would help your people, don't you think he might be right?"

"Like betrothals," she said with forced confidence. "Just because something worked in the past doesn't mean it's the only option now." Treasure would make her father see reason.

Because she couldn't imagine a life without Teo.

He looked at her curiously. "You really don't know anything about who your betrothed is?"

She shook her head vigorously. "Absolutely not. I'm sure my father had mentioned details to me in the past, but I've done everything I could to shut that out of my life. Like if I refused to know anything about the situation, it couldn't actually exist."

He sat back in his seat while the plane took to the air. Treasure waited until her ears adjusted to the cabin pressure and the plane leveled off before asking, "Do you know anything about your princess?"

"I do," he admitted. "At first, I'd been opposed to the idea, but I always had a vague sort of curiosity about it. About her. Since taking the throne, I'd come around to the idea a bit."

A horrible thought occurred to her. Had last night been a fling, despite their exchange of pretty words? "But, even after last night?"

The seatbelt light went off, and before Teo could answer, the flight attendant appeared. "What can I get you both?" she asked.

"I'll have a cup of coffee and a mimosa," Treasure answered.

"Certainly. And for you, sir?"

"I'll have the same."

Treasure kept her eyes on the flight attendant as she started the coffee maker, then started mixing the Cointreau, fresh orange juice, and champagne.

It was easier to keep her eyes averted than to look at Teo and acknowledge the question that was left hanging between them.

It seemed to be an achingly long time before she returned with a tray and placed their mugs of coffee and their champagne flutes down in front of them, followed by cream and sugar servings.

"If you need anything else, just buzz me. There's also the bedroom back there, ready for when you want to relax on the flight. If you need anything, just ring the button. Otherwise, I'll leave you alone." The woman winked, and Treasure forced herself to return the smile.

When the flight attendant returned to the crew area, Teo lifted his mimosa to Treasure. "I'd like to propose a toast."

"What are we toasting to?"

"Us finding each other. How's that?"

Treasure smiled and clinked her glass with his. "To us."

They both took a sip, and then Teo unbuckled his seat belt and leaned forward, taking Treasure's hands in his. "About last night. I never intended to take things that far, despite how much I wanted you. In fact, *because* I feel so strongly about you, I'd wanted to take things slow. Especially since you expressed that you wanted things to stay professional."

Treasure's heart sank. "You regret what happened," she stated.

"No!" He moved from his seat across from her and slid into the one beside her, cupping her cheek, "I don't regret a thing about last night, and you shouldn't either."

She palmed his hand. "Even so, we need to put that aside. I can't be distracted. Once we land, there will be too many eyes on me. I need us to go back to professional-only."

Something flickered in Teo's eyes. Regret? Relief? Treasure couldn't tell. "Okay, we can do that."

"Thank you."

"Although we haven't landed yet. And it will be quite some time before we do." He raised an eyebrow with his proposition.

"And she did say she'd leave us alone unless we called for her," Treasure added, looking toward the crew area before biting her bottom lip and gazing into his darkening eyes.

His arm snaked around her as his lips crashed onto hers. They were attentive, yet needy. She parted her lips for him, and he explored every inch of her mouth.

Treasure desperately wanted to commit his taste to memory, especially knowing it would be the last time she'd be able to kiss him once they landed.

Or maybe ever... if I can't convince my father to release me from the betrothal.

She pushed that thought out of her mind, focusing instead on the tiny kisses he pressed down her neck until he found her soft spot, the one that made her moan with pleasure.

Passion fueled them as she moved onto his lap, pressing herself against his growing erection, the tip of him teasing her femininity with pleasure. She ground her hips into him with a steady rocking motion, sending heat throughout her body. His mouth latched onto her neck as the pleasure rose.

She cried out when his teeth bore down on her flesh.

Then suddenly, he broke away from her, leaving her body feeling cold without his heat as he held her back at a distance.

"Baby," he said as he slid her off of him and guided her gently back into her seat.

"What?" she asked, bewildered.

"Your speech. You haven't written it yet."

"Ugh," she groaned, tossing her head back against the headrest. "Just when you think you've got a free morning to satiate your personal desires, the royal duty sneaks up to strangle you before your feet even touch down on homeland."

"Treasure," he said softly. "It's not all that bad. I just remembered about it, and I think you should focus on that before I distract you. I'd never forgive myself if you arrived at the talks unprepared."

"Right," Treasure moaned, dropping her face into her hands. "You're right. It's just that going home stresses me out, and thinking about that speech gives me total anxiety."

"Why?" he asked, placing an arm around her.

"Because all my life I've been trying to live up to my father's expectations, and every time I think I might be able to, he winds up piling more and more on me, proving nothing I do will ever be good enough."

"I'm sure that's not true..." He tried to soothe her.

"It is," she replied, lifting her head from her hands to look at him. "When I graduated salutatorian in high school, he said I should have graduated valedictorian. If I won a silver at my school's sporting games, I should have gotten gold. To him, being the best symbolized strength, and no matter how hard I tried, I was never able to be as great as he wished I was."

"He wanted to instill excellence in you. My father was similar with me. But that doesn't mean you're not good enough. It doesn't mean a speech you put your best into won't please him."

"I don't think you understand." She shook her head. "Now that my father is looking at retirement, I'm *terrified*. Not just of his opinion but of everyone else's too. He's been such a great leader for our island for centuries, and I don't know if I can lead in his place."

"But I *do* understand. There are times I feel the same way about my territory. But it gets better. Easier. You'll become used to leading, and before you know it, you'll come into your own way of ruling, without the shadow of the previous ruler's legacy looming over you. He's created a foundation, but it's not a mold for you to fit into. It's a place for you to step off from, just like he did when he took the crown from the ruler before them, and that rule from the one before them, and on back through time. You're just the next piece—albeit an important piece—in the big puzzle, and you're allowed to be your own shape. That's the most important thing to remember in all of this."

"Wow, you really have a way with words." She swallowed hard while tears prickled her eyes. "And that's what I mean. I don't think I can motivate my people with such eloquent speeches like that."

"It wasn't always that easy for me to speak so eloquently. It came with time, and it will come to you too. I mean you graduated salutatorian! At some point, you must have taken an English or speech class. You'll have the words," he said with a wink.

"Yeah… English *was* my favorite subject. I loved writing research papers and even short stories… but that's completely different than speeches when you're expected to be clever and argue your point."

"Treasure, you have the gift of gab. I've seen it in our short time together. You're so bright, intriguing, and easy to talk to. I see that, and your people will too. I believe in you, baby. I really do."

She offered him a reluctant smile. "Well, I'm glad one of us is confident in me."

"I'll always, always be your cheerleader." He kissed her temple and then pressed the call button.

The flight attendant appeared instantly. "What can I help you with?" she asked.

"Can we get some paper and pens? We have some work to do."

After a heavy round of brainstorming, Treasure needed a break. "That bed back there is calling me," she proclaimed, carefully folding her notes and placing them into her handbag.

She stood and stretched, and Teo snaked an arm around her and pulled her to his chest. "Mind if I come with you?"

"I wouldn't be happy any other way." She kissed him then turned and led the way to the small room that housed a small desk, a chair, and a bed.

"Do you want to get a little more sleep since we didn't get much last night?" she asked.

"I'm not thinking about sleep right now, babe." His gaze locked onto hers as he palmed her shoulders.

"I was hoping you'd say that."

She stood still, allowing him to slowly and gracefully strip her of her clothes then pull back the covers on the bed before scooping her up and placing her on it. She waited while he removed his clothing, and her body sang when he climbed in next to her.

"I've fallen for you, Treasure. I hope you know that," he said as he caressed her cheek.

Treasure smiled and pulled him close to her. "I'm falling for you too." Her lips gently brushed his collarbone before gliding up to his neck toward his earlobe.

He let out a low growl in response and brushed his hands over her body until she nearly couldn't take it anymore, until he finally settled over her and plunged his length within her. He rocked her core until she came undone beneath him, and then the two fell into a blissful sleep for the next several hours of flight.

8

———

The intercom woke them.

We're nearing the island of Milos. Please return to your seats and safely buckle in for our descent.

Reluctantly, they pried themselves from each other's arms, dressed, and found their way back to their seats.

Teo enjoyed watching Treasure touch up her makeup and smooth down her hair, though one thought haunted him.

He'd been unable to contact anyone to ensure his secret would be kept.

He tried calling his father before they left Treasure's condo, but his father's assistant insisted he was unreachable but assured him they were in contact with the pilot, so his father would know when he was on his way.

He woke up on the plane and snuck away while Treasure slept, and despite trying to reach both of their fathers and saying it was an urgent matter, they wouldn't take his calls.

Teo knew *exactly* why.

Because the kings had set the two of them up, and neither wanted to hear any complaints about it.

He *had* to make sure no one mentioned the betrothal. He had to get to the kings first before Treasure found out the truth. Despite their feelings for each other, Treasure was strong-willed, and she had her mind set on the fact that she didn't want the betrothal.

If she found out, he wouldn't be able to convince her that his feelings for her were real. She'd think she'd been tricked. That he seduced her and made her fall for him under false pretenses.

What had he done? He'd messed up royally... If she knew he knew and still slept with her, it wouldn't matter that he'd just gotten carried away...

As the pilot droned on about the weather on Milos, Treasure placed her bag under her seat. "Not long now," she said cheerfully.

"Not long at all." He gave her a smile, though he knew it didn't reach his eyes. Here this woman was so hopeful. She was preparing to be courageous and face her father.

And he was dreading facing reality.

"I mean it," she said. "I don't want to hide this from my father. As soon as we land, I'm telling him that I want to be with you and not the person he promised me to."

"Are you sure?" Teo asked. "I mean we have the talks ahead of us. Maybe it would be better to get through that first, focus on the security, and then approach our relationship after that."

Treasure frowned, knitting her eyebrows. "I know I said I want to maintain professionalism during the talks, but I still need to confront my father right away. For years he's been trying to force me to meet this guy, and I *know* he's going to try to force him on me during the talks. Unless I can convince him to dissolve it."

"Right," Teo said, taking a deep breath.

"He's always wanted to see my strength. Well, here it is. I'm going to inherit a kingdom soon, and I want to be a powerful leader, so it starts with standing up to my father about this."

Teo smiled nervously. The news of him being her betrothed would devastate her. He had to get to both fathers before she found out the truth. He just hoped he could do it before it was too late.

He had to figure out a way to distract her so he could get the two kings alone before it was too late.

Unfortunately, that didn't happen.

Treasure chewed on her bottom lip. Her time at FUCN'A had been the first and only time in her life when she'd lived free from her palace responsibilities.

She'd been able to move around with her peers and the FUC agents, free from BS shadowing her every move—a way of life she truly enjoyed. Bonafide Security always had the annoying knack of letting her know which rules of princess etiquette she broke, but while in Canada, she didn't have to appear as the embodiment of perfect royalty in front of all of her people.

She envied people like Harriet, who had taken to her royal duties like a duck to water. Harriet fit right into her role of being the Queen of Skyros, and almost the instant after she married her cousin Lear, too. Was it because the Hare didn't have the weight of expectations? Or did some people just have a more natural knack for leading?

As they disembarked from the jet, they were greeted by both of their fathers. King Ambrose instantly drew Treasure into his arms. "It's so good to see you, my darling daughter. How was the flight?"

"It was good, Father," she replied, waiting a moment after he released her to broach the subject. "Before we are focused on the talks, I need to discuss something with you."

"Do you?" Her father looked from her to Teo with a smile that looked like he was nearly bursting at the seams with joy. She'd never seen him looking so jolly. *Strange.*

"Yes, well, actually"—she took Teo's hand in hers—"there's something we'd both like to discuss with you."

"Treasure," Teo said, "could we wait until we're at the palace, maybe?"

Teo's words were almost drowned out by his father's voice. "Teo! You finally captured your betrothed!"

Treasure turned her head, expecting to see Teo's betrothed among the others assembled, but no one stepped forward from the group of assistants and drivers.

Her confusion grew when her father added, "We knew this would all work out if we had you meet in the Rockies. We must thank Stan properly for helping arrange it all."

She saw her father's wink, but her head was swimming. What were they saying?

The realization came to her when she saw the horrified look on Teo's face. "Treasure, I'm sorry."

She felt her head grow hot. "No," she whispered.

She'd spent her whole life refusing to meet her betrothed, watching out for her father's tricks. She'd locked herself in her room, employed hunger strikes, and even threatened to walk away from public appearances whenever she caught on to his ploys.

But at FUCN'A, her guard had been down.

She should have seen this coming! She should have *known* not to trust Mateo Abara, a king who was going to the talks and was stopping by WANC for *one afternoon.*

"Treasure, let me explain," Teo started, but she stopped him by ripping her hand from his and holding it up before her.

Now she knew the truth, and *nothing* he could say could fix it.

They'd taken away her right to make her own choice.

The three men in front of her.

The anger built up inside her like an active volcano getting ready to erupt, and she felt it attacking the mating bond she had with Teo, weakening anything she'd thought might be there.

He must have felt it, too, because his face became more pained with each passing second.

"You lied to me from the first moment you walked into that office." She nearly spat the words as she locked eyes with him, daring Teo to try to lie his way out of it.

"Treasure, it's not like that. I promise—"

"Oh, I'm pretty sure I've heard more than enough about your promises."

"Please, let me explain!" Teo begged as he placed his arms on her shoulders. "We need to fix this."

"We don't need to do anything of the sort. My only obligation to you is to ensure your security detail during the talks. Now please let me go before I say something BS will make me regret. The press is already waiting outside the gates, and I want to avoid rumors flying around before the SHIT starts," she said to him as she took his hands off her shoulders.

She then looked over at her father. "I trust Dayton has the car ready?"

"He should, dear. But you're expected to greet the press before we leave for the palace. Our people are excited about your return."

"Then you can have one of the staff explain to them that the jet lag is troubling me. Inform them that I'm expected to rest for the afternoon and will endeavor to greet them in the gardens tonight, before dinner."

The staff looked from her to her father for approval. "If that is how she wishes to address her people, far be it from me to object. After all, she will be queen shortly."

Teo watched helplessly as the driver helped Treasure into her car while another staff member walked down the laid-out carpet toward the press at the gates.

"That girl will be the death of me. I am certain of it," King Ambrose said with a sigh before turning to face Teo. "What happened while you both were at Furry United Coalition Newbie Academy?"

Remembering that there were observers, Teo

kept his composure. "I attempted to contact both of you to give you warning, and you both refused my calls."

The kings exchanged a look before Teo continued. "How could you do this to us? How could you lie to us both? Once I figured it out, I was afraid to tell her because I knew this would happen. If only one of you had taken my calls, I could have warned you not to say anything."

"You wanted to keep her in the dark?" his father asked.

"Yes—no! I don't know." Teo ran a hand through his hair. "That's just it. You put me in an impossible situation. Had I told her while I was there, she would have shut me out, just like she is now."

"I'll talk to her," King Ambrose promised. "Treasure is strong-willed, but she can be made to see reason. There is, after all, a contract involved."

Teo shook his head. "Nothing we can say will make her believe that I wasn't in on this 'chance' meeting too."

"Excuse me, Your Highnesses?" A BS agent with her hand to the headset in her ear stepped forward. "We're getting word that we need to get you into the cars and return to the palace immediately. There is a potential Zagan sitting on the island."

"Really?" King Solomon asked with widened eyes.

"Let's get you all to safety."

Both King Solomon and King Ambrose took the car with Teo, each wanting to learn more about what had happened between their children.

"You were holding hands when you stepped off the jet," King Solomon stated once the car began moving. "Does that mean things had gone well?"

Teo shook his head. "I'm not getting into it with either of you. I think you've both done enough. I'll need to come up with a plan to fix it from here."

They rode in silence the rest of the way. It wasn't long before they were pulling up the long driveway that led to the enormous estate. The grand home was a winter white stucco with a salmon-colored clay roof with gardens that seemed to stretch for kilometers. Every little inch of greenery in the gardens had a different theme and colored flowers. Some were bright yellows, others lilacs, and even a hint of red was splashed in between some white flowers in a secluded section of the property.

Teo's mouth gaped open at the sight of the property. His island off Madagascar was beautiful with its own greenery and gorgeous red, purple, and orange sunsets. But the scene he was taking in was beyond breathtaking.

Everywhere his eyes gazed, he saw beauty.

And Treasure.

He hoped it wasn't too late to fix things between them.

He just had to figure out how.

9

———

Treasure paced back and forth in her room, frustrated that her homecoming had been ruined. Now, instead of finding her sisters, Lear, and Harriet, she was holed up in her room, hiding from them all.

How could Teo have lied to me? Well, it wasn't really a lie. Was it? I guess it's more like an omission. And maybe it's not really that either? I mean we did just meet a couple of days ago, so it's not like he could tell me everything about himself...

"Ugh! Who am I kidding! He lied! And he probably did it so I wouldn't get pissed at him!" She plopped onto her bed and punched a fist into her pillow.

"You're right. I was afraid to."

Treasure jumped up to see Teo standing in her

doorway. "How did you get into my apartment?" she demanded, marching toward him and forcing him to retreat from her bedroom into her sitting room.

She slammed her room door behind her, as though keeping him out of her inner sanctum could keep him at a distance.

"I have my ways," he replied, taking a seat on her sofa as though nothing was wrong.

"Well, when I find out who let you in, I'm going to have them fired," she replied with gritted teeth. "Get off my couch and leave my apartments immediately."

He ignored her directions. "I debated about it all yesterday, all night, the whole time on the plane. I couldn't figure out a way to do it that wouldn't lead to losing you."

She didn't want to argue with him. She didn't want to give him a chance to use his words to soothe her anger. "I'll call the guards," she threatened.

"Will you, though?" He raised an eyebrow. "Why, exactly? Are you afraid if you give me a chance, your resolve will melt?"

When she didn't reply, he continued. "Of course you are. Because I know how you feel about me. You have your pride and your stubbornness, and right now, they're at war with your heart. With your feelings for me."

"Don't presume to know me," she snapped.

He gave a low laugh. "Then prove me wrong. If you're not afraid of losing your resolve, then you'll have no problem having a discussion with me. We are, after all, leaders of allied nations. This is bigger than you and me. We must find a way to be copacetic for the sake of our kingdoms."

She set her jaw as she took a seat at her meeting table and indicated the chair across from her. "Fine."

He moved from the couch to the table, taking a seat as any other dignitary would. "Princess Garner of the Island of Milos, despite your mistrust of me at the moment, I swear to you I did not conspire to deceive you. I was not any part of the plan between our fathers and Stan of FUCN'A."

He didn't beg her to believe him, a fact she appreciated. She couldn't stand groveling. "Say I believe you—that you weren't in on it. I'm not saying I do. I'm just asking, if I *did*, then when did you figure it out, and why should I forgive you for not telling me at that moment?"

"First, I need you to know that when I walked into your office, I did *not* know who you were, but I was instantly struck on an extremely deep level. It was only when I learned your name and where you were from that I feared I knew the truth, though I hoped maybe you were one of the younger princesses of Milos. Once you confirmed you were heir, I knew what my father had done."

"So, pretty much from the beginning of our meeting then?"

He nodded. "Yes, and at first, I said nothing because we had a job to do. We were looking into the security plans—something that was very important to me and also seemed important to you. I knew if I told you then it would disrupt our meeting. Plus, I kept wondering if you knew. I was sure you had to know. So I said nothing, and you said nothing, so I just went forward with the meeting."

"That's why you kept asking me if I knew the name of my betrothed," she mused. "Even when we first boarded the jet."

"Yes," he agreed. "I guess it was how I was justifying my actions. I'd just lost myself with you. I let myself get swept away in the intense feelings I had. I shouldn't have. I should have told you. I know I should have, but I was so afraid you'd shut me out. And you would have, you know you would have."

"Probably," she confirmed.

"And then we both would have missed out on experiencing what we had between us. Yes, I committed a lie of omission, but I can't say I regret it if it was the only chance I had of getting a few moments with you."

Treasure blinked and tried to swallow the lump in her throat. She didn't want to let him off the hook so easily, but was pride and stubbornness really worth losing him? "I really wish this would have gone differently."

"I can understand that. I feel the same way, and honestly, lying to you gutted me. But I was so afraid of losing you."

Treasure looked into his eyes and was startled when she saw they had changed. Instead of the clear blue of the ocean, they were now intense, almost indigo pools staring back at her. The longer she maintained eye contact, the more her fears and trepidations dissipated.

As well as her obstinance.

Was this really the stand she wanted to take?

She'd deny herself a potential lifetime of love just to spite her father?

A sense of calm washed over her as the Aegean Sea, in the form of Teo's eyes, sat before her. He must have sensed the change in her because he stood and approached her, slowly inching closer until their lips were a breath apart.

"Treasure, I hope you can forgive me. I didn't intend to lie to you. I care about you so much. I mean I'm falling in love with you." He pulled both of her hands into his as he knelt before her.

She sighed, finally relenting. "Say we forget our fathers and our territories for a moment and only talk about us. As in, where do we go from here?"

"I still want you, Treasure. That will never change."

"Teo," she said as she took her hands from his, stood, and stepped away from the table. "The truth is, I don't know where we go from here, and we really don't have time to figure it out right now. I need to get my mind in a place where I can focus on the talks and on my part in security."

"I understand," he said as he sat on the bed. "For what it's worth, I truly am sorry."

"I believe you. I can see it in your eyes."

"Okay." Teo nodded, standing slowly and following her to the door.

She waited for him to walk a few paces before she gave a look to the FUC and BS agents stationed at her door. "You let anyone else in here without my permission and I'll make you wish you'd been a failed Mastermind project."

Treasure enjoyed an uninterrupted nap, and though she woke up with Teo's lies still weighing on her mind, she at least felt refreshed enough to get ready to meet the press.

She changed into a new A-line dress, reapplied her makeup, and tamed her hair.

A part of her wanted to talk to Teo, but her thoughts were a mess. If they could get through the talks, then she could take some time to herself to try to sort everything out.

Until then, she had to stay focused.

She donned her headpiece and spoke into it to test it, making sure she'd have direct access to the security teams while she was on the ground. Once she confirmed it was working, she combed her hair over her ear, effectively hiding the small device.

Her FUC and BS agents followed her to the garden, where she stood at the podium and answered questions from the press.

"What designer are you wearing?"

"How has your training with FUC been going?"

"What do you miss most about the island when you're gone?"

"Have you met the famous Miranda or Viktor while at FUCN'A?"

"Are you ready for the talks?"

"Have you had a chance to visit with King Lear and Queen Harriet yet?"

"Do you think Zagan is going to make a move during the talks?"

"Are you and King Teo an item?"

She handled all the questions with ease until Zagan and Teo were brought up, but she was prepared for it. She gave a "no comment" on the Zagan question, and at Teo's name, she gave the signal to her aide, who replaced her at the podium. "Unfortunately, Princess Treasure is due for her entrance at dinner. Thank you all for your questions!"

10

Treasure made it through dinner without any problems—from Zagan or Teo.

A part of her had hoped that she'd end up with Teo at her table, but she didn't even catch sight of him. Instead, she sat with her sisters, Lear, and Harriet, interspersed with other visiting dignitaries.

To their credit, her family kept the conversation on light topics, not even bringing up the rumors of her tryst with Teo, which had quickly spread through the palace.

When the meal was over, and they all rose from the dining table, Treasure excused herself, citing the eighteen-hour flight as the reason for her need to retire early and skip the rest of the evening's activities.

With one agent walking ahead of her and the other behind, she almost didn't see the figure waiting at the door to her apartment.

"Teo?"

The agents looked to her for instruction. "It's fine," she said. "I'll talk to him."

"May I come in?" he asked.

"Sure," she said, sighing as she unlocked and opened her door.

Once inside, with the door shut behind them, she removed her FUC earpiece, turning the device off and setting it on the table before turning to face Teo.

"I'm sure you are still upset—" he started.

"Teo, I'm not even thinking about that," she fibbed. *I'm at least trying not to think about it.*

"Of course you're not. You're focused on your duty and all the pressures that come with it. Might I be so bold to say, though, that you're doing magnificently? I watched you handle the press in the garden with such poise and grace, and you looked absolutely elegant. If I didn't know any better, I'd think you were absolutely carefree."

"Maybe I am," she replied, slipping off her shoes and taking them to her closet.

"Well, then I'm glad you were able to overcome

all the fears of inadequacy that you expressed to me before. All your nerves of the talks. Your intimidation of stepping into your father's role."

She tossed him a glare. "I don't appreciate your assumption of familiarity toward me."

"Come on, Treasure." He walked over to her and placed his hand on her shoulder. "Don't push me away. I don't want to be separated from you tonight —especially not with a Zagan sighting earlier today. Let me stay with you. Let me hold you in my arms."

Would it really be so bad to take him up on his offer? She sighed. "I want to do things right for my people and my father, and despite all of what happened, I still care. I don't think I could *ever* stop caring about you."

"Yeah?" he asked, a sparkle returning to his eyes.

She nodded. "I think I'd very much like my rock beside me during the talks."

He pulled her into his arms, kissing her firmly as though they'd been separated for years, not just hours. "Really?" he asked when they came up for air. "You're certain?"

"Yes. In the time I spent without you by my side, I realized how wrong that felt. We're meant to be together, and I know you weren't in on our fathers' plan to set us up. Somehow, we managed to fall for each other despite all the interfering. That counts for something."

He held her tight and kissed the top of her head. "Yes, that definitely counts for something."

"We still need to focus on the talks. Protect the dignitaries from Zagan."

"And we're stronger together, as a team."

Treasure awoke to a series of loud bangs.

"Gunshots!" Teo sprang from the bed as quickly as she did, and they emerged from the bedroom as the security team entered the apartment.

"What's going on?" Treasure asked, sliding a robe over her nightgown.

"Shots fired in the palace. All lockdown security measures are being taken," the FUC agent said as he ran to the window, his gun in hand.

"We need you two to get to the center of the room," the BS agent instructed, pushing past them and scouting Treasure's bedroom.

"I don't think so," Treasure said, ducking into her closet, emerging with an outfit over her arm, and then shutting herself in her bathroom.

Teo knew what she had in mind, and he threw

on his jeans and T-shirt, glad he'd dressed down before visiting Treasure after dinner.

Treasure quickly emerged, grabbing her FUC headset off the table and hooking it to her ear before leaving her quarters. "You all can stay here or follow me, but I won't be staying inside."

"I'm right behind you," Teo said, tossing a glance to the agents. "You're to guard us, right?"

Their objections were lost to an empty room, as Treasure had started down the hallway in a run and Teo followed right behind her.

"Princess Treasure! King Mateo!" A large group of security guards had taken position on the bridge outside Treasure's wing. "We need you to stay in your quarters."

"Negative," Treasure responded. "Teo and I are part of the security team. Now, give me a status update on my sisters and our fathers."

"Your sisters are all secured," the lead agent replied, clearly not liking Treasure's refusal to listen to orders but knowing Treasure spoke the truth. "King Solomon is also accounted for."

"Where is my father?" Treasure snapped, her gaze sliding over the group of agents. When no one answered, she demanded, "What happened?"

"It was a surprise attack by Zagan and his

cronies. A maid witnessed them taking King Ambrose."

Treasure froze. "Which way did they go? I assume a team is searching the grounds?"

"Of course, Princess."

Teo patted her shoulder. "They will find him, I'm sure of it."

"We have to cancel the talks." Treasure turned to look at him. "We should have already done that. We have to send home all the dignitaries who've already arrived and turn back any others still on their way."

"Hold on, Treasure. First, let's focus on the search for your father, and we can worry about the rest later."

Treasure sighed and wrung her hands. "With Father gone, *I'm* in charge."

He nodded. "And if he were here, what would he tell you to do?"

She sighed, closing her eyes and hearing exactly what he'd say to her. "He'd want the talks to continue as planned. He'd tell me to keep the talks going and not to cancel them. It would show a sign of strength on our part that Zagan can't defeat us."

No sooner had she made her decision when a voice spoke up through the headsets. "King Ambrose has been found!"

"Where is he now?" Treasure demanded, holding her hand to her ear so she wouldn't miss a word.

"We're returning him to his room at once."

"And Zagan?"

"Gone."

"Drat," Treasure sighed then turned to the guards around her. "Let me through. I must attend to my father."

She hadn't asked about his status over the comms link—if he were incapacitated, it wasn't something they would want advertised to everyone listening.

The minute it took her to run to his room felt like an eternity, though she saw the team that recovered him had beat her there. Before she entered, she looked at Teo and accepted his hand, grateful for the comforting squeeze he offered her.

She stepped through the door to the king's chambers and found a team surrounding her father's bed. "How is he?" she asked, making her way to his bedside and finding him to look asleep.

"Zagan administered some kind of concoction, and I've been unable to wake him," Galen, one of the lead guards of the palace, answered her.

Treasure took the seat she was offered by her father's side. "The physician has been called?" she asked as she stroked his hand, and her breath grew shallow and sporadic.

"Yes, we have. He's on his way."

Treasure nodded. "Please, leave us for a moment."

The guards and security agents exited the room, leaving Treasure and Teo alone with the unconscious king.

"What am I going to do, Teo? I said I'd let the talks go on, but I can't take his place. What will I say? He has to wake up. He just has to!"

"You said it yourself that he would want the talks to continue, so let's make that happen."

"But, Teo—"

"But nothing! Now is the time for action, not fear. We've very little time for you to prepare for what you need to do, so let's not waste any of that precious time dwelling in doubt. Zagan is still out there, and if he got through all our security once, he could do it again. So we'll sit right here, and we'll prepare and plan, and when the time comes, you'll go out there and you'll be the leader everyone needs you to be."

New voices in the hallway brightened Treasure's spirits, and she flew from her chair to catch Lear and Harriet in a hug. "Thank you for coming."

"It was almost impossible to get past our guards,

but we heard what happened and knew you needed us," Harriet said before catching sight of Teo. "Hi, I'm Harriet, and this is Lear, and I already know you must be Teo."

"Word gets around," Teo replied, shaking hands with both of them.

"We're not here just for moral support," Lear said. "I want to tell you about some technological advances in security my team has been developing."

Treasure sighed in relief. "Yes, please tell me all about it. We need everything possible."

Harriet and Lear briefed Treasure and Teo on the drones they brought with them, great for aerial and perimeter surveillance, and Treasure's spirits lifted. "That sounds like exactly what we need."

Her heart soared even more when her father made a low mumbling sound.

"Father, I am here," she said, quickly returning to his side.

But the mumbling stopped as quickly as it came. The king was still unconscious.

Treasure sighed. "What if he doesn't ever wake up?"

"He will," Teo replied, and Harriet and Lear nodded in agreement.

"We found a way to thwart Zagan when he

kidnapped my father and Stan," Lear said. "Everything turned out fine then, and it will now too."

"Zagan's been injecting lemurs in Madagascar with serums, and while it inhibits their shifting ability for a while, we've been able to treat them, and they've all at least regained consciousness."

Treasure heard what he didn't say—they didn't all re-gain their ability to shift. *What if father wakes up but can never shift into a leatherback and enjoy the ocean again? What kind of life is that?*

Finally, the physician appeared in the doorway. "I got here as fast as I could. Would you all mind clearing the room so I can run tests on him? Except for security, of course."

Treasure and the others nodded and filtered out of the room as the doctor and several FUC and BS agents entered. "The FUC agents know what happened to King Gregor last year. They'll know what they need to test my father for."

"And the BS agents know what we've seen in the lemurs," Teo assured her.

The sun was already rising on Milos, which meant they were closer to the beginning of the talks.

"We can do this," Treasure said, more to convince herself than the others. "We won't let Zagan destroy us."

11

As more dignitaries and guests arrived for the talks, Treasure and Teo worked overtime on all areas of operations—but mostly on security.

It had been a long afternoon of planning before the welcome home dinner. Treasure was still uncertain as to whether or not all the details would come to fruition. There hadn't been any changes in her father's condition, and he was officially the worst and longest case caused by Zagan's concoction that any FUC or BS had seen up to this point.

All of the security and operations planning, plus worries about her father, plus making a show here and there to greet certain VIPs, meant Treasure had found no time to plan out her welcome speech for the evening. She was riddled with great uncertainty as to what to say to the people at the dinner.

She needed to address her father's condition without sounding so dire that the people would fear for the king or doubt their own safety at the talks. Her father was always better at this delicate balancing act than she was. She was grateful she had Teo's, Lear's, and Harriet's help, but everything that they'd come up with so far fell flat.

"We have to come up with something that will make the people of Milos feel safe and secure, and I'm really not sure how to convey that," Treasure said as she paced the floor of her bedroom. She let out a sigh before continuing. "Before tonight, the only thing I worried about with events like these was what I was going to wear. God! I wish my father could speak. He'd have the right thing to say!"

"Treasure, I really think you are making this out to be more difficult than it has to be," Harriet reassured her. "Just be as truthful as you can without giving away too much."

Treasure let out a sigh. "But everything just sounds like someone else is making a statement and not me."

"That's because you keep coming up with something your father would say and not what you would say," Teo replied, walking over to her and wrapping his arms around her from behind. His defined shoulders, tightened around her smaller frame, signified a sense of warmth and safety. If only she could offer the same to her people in the form of her speech.

My people.

It was the first time she had ever considered the people of Milos as *hers*. Up until that point, she always found her palace duties unimportant. She enjoyed her charity work. That was something rewarding. But banquet and auction planning for specific charities was the part of her duties she hated the most.

That was probably the main reason why she'd been struggling for so long. No one had truly prepared her for this moment. The moment she needed to be the one to lead. And all of this struggling was because her father still thought of her as a fragile little girl that needed protection.

"Treasure, close your eyes and picture what it is that you want to say to the people of Milos," Teo said to her as he kissed the top of her head.

Both Lear and Harriet shot a look at each other as they watched the pair embrace, but they both stayed silent, allowing Treasure and Teo their moment.

"I want to tell them that father fell ill several days ago, that we're confident of his recovery, but he's not currently able to attend the talk or any related festivities. And, of course, that I will be taking his place, as has always been his wish."

"Okay, that's a good start, but what will you say if reporters press the issue about your father's condition and want more information as to why he's fallen ill?" Harriet asked.

Treasure shook her head and broke free from Teo's arms. "This is exactly where I fall short because I have no idea what to say. And if I can't address the press with authority, I have no business ruling the island," Treasure said with a long breath. "Face it, I'm just not any good at this. And not for nothing—we are assuming the press doesn't know about Zagan almost kidnapping the king. What if one of them already knows? I mean, *DAMN*. That wouldn't be good."

"We will come up with something, babe. Just try to relax," Teo said.

She turned to face him. "No, I mean the Diarist Authors and Milos Newspersons—DAMN. They are like psychics. They always seem to know stuff before we all do. It's possible they caught wind of the poten-tial kidnapping already."

Teo cupped her face. "Close your eyes again," he said, lulling her back to a state of calm with his silky voice.

"Why?"

"Because you *are* capable of handling this. You *have* had training all your life for this moment. Now, you can concentrate on what's in your heart and not what is on your notecards."

"Fine," she sighed as she closed her eyes.

"Clear your mind of everything that's happened in the past twenty-four hours and just think about how to respond to the question of your father's condition and the kidnapping."

Treasure took a couple of deep breaths before responding. "My people of Milos, I have every inten-tion of protecting you from Zagan. In addition to the tutelage under the very best that Milos Island's Bonafide Security has to offer, I've now also trained with the best-of-the-best of the Furry United Coali-tion agents. I will not let you all down. Now, both agencies are here on the island and on high alert, and we will continue the SHIT, just as King Ambrose would."

She opened her eyes. Teo kissed her on both

cheeks. "I couldn't have said that better myself! See? You can do it, Treasure!"

Treasure reached for her pen and frantically started writing down what she had just uttered. Teo took the pen from her, saying, "Babe, you don't have to say it word for word. In fact, it's probably best you don't come out with notecards tonight. You don't want to appear rehearsed. You want to show that natural confidence."

"You're right. I'll try to shoot from the hip." She took in another deep breath to calm her pounding heart.

"Treasure, you are going to be great. I am certain of it," Teo said.

"Please sit beside me. Because if things go south, I'll need my rock by my side."

"Always," he said as he squeezed her hand.

"Well, I'd better get ready for tonight. I'm going to have even more security than usual. Guards for the princess, guards for the crown jewels... guards for the current leader of Milos..."

***

Teo and Treasure left the room, and Harriet turned to Lear. "I've clearly missed something."

"Don't look at me," Lear replied. "Treasure's betrothal and love life were well beyond my scope of influence."

"Last I heard whispers of it, they'd had a falling out?"

"Sure, you would have heard more than I would have."

Harriet shook her head, staring thoughtfully out the window. "But it's obvious they're in love."

"I don't know what's going on between the two of them. Maybe we will find out more tonight."

Treasure had a team ready for her when she returned to her room. She sat for her hair and makeup and then stepped into a gorgeous amber-brown gown, a combination of a satin bodice and layered tulle beaded with silver sequins.

An aide helped her into a matching pair of satin shoes, and then the security that specifically guarded the crown jewels opened several boxes for her to choose from.

She picked an emerald and diamond tiara, which felt much heavier on her head than normal, and a set of earrings and necklace to match. They'd all belonged to her mother.

Once they were on, she asked everyone to step out of her bedroom for a moment.

Alone, she looked in the full-length mirror and tried adjusting the tiara. The weight fully felt like the weight of the kingdom on her head.

When she put her hands down and took in her full image, she gasped. *That is my mother staring back at me!*

Treasure had not expected the full-grown adult staring back at her in the mirror, and it made her feel worse—even more of an imposter.

But it didn't matter what she saw or how she felt. What mattered was what she had to do for her people and what *they* would see when they looked at her.

"I'm going to try to make you proud, Father."

And Teo.

He was intrinsically linked to her now, that much she knew for sure. She was walking into her new role that evening, but she didn't have to do it alone. She had her mate at her side.

Despite all of her resistance in her younger years, her father had been right. Teo was exactly what Treasure needed in her life. He gave her a sense of safety, and he was the confidant she needed, especially now that she couldn't speak with her father.

A knock on her bedroom door was followed by Teo's voice. "You almost ready, babe?"

"I am," she said, opening the door to her sitting room, where Teo waited with all of their guards.

Teo's eyes widened. "You look absolutely stunning," he said as he offered her his elbow.

"Can I ask you something before we head down?"

"Certainly."

"I was thinking... how would you feel about making this dinner more about announcing our union than about Father's illness? Of course I'll need to address his absence, but if we let them know about the alliance between the Madagascar rock agamas and the Milos leatherbacks, it may give them a good reason to celebrate."

Teo cupped her face and searched her eyes. "Are you sure about this? Because, as much as I know nothing would make me happier than having you as my forever mate, I don't want you to feel pressured into that commitment because you're trying to give your people a reason for hope."

"I am sure. I don't need to discuss it with our

fathers—they know what they did. And we know that we don't appreciate being tricked, but we *were* meant to be together. I shouldn't have been so stubborn, but we all make mistakes. Now, I want to move forward, with you by my side, starting tonight."

Teo nodded. "All right. Then I can definitely accommodate." He removed his hands from her face and pulled out a small box from his jacket pocket.

The others in the room gasped, and time seemed to move in slow motion as Teo dropped to a knee while he opened the box to reveal an oval sapphire encased in diamonds.

"This ring was my mother's, and I bring it with me when I travel, to keep her spirit close within my heart. I always hoped I'd find my mate—the person who would capture my heart—and that I could someday give her the ring and keep her close to me instead. Treasure, I can't believe we've finally met, and how it turns out we were really meant to be. I *truly* love you. Will you marry me?"

Treasure nodded, tears welling up in her eyes. "Yes, Teo, I'll marry you."

He gave her a crooked smile. "Last chance... you sure? Do you really want to do this?"

She took his hands and pulled him back to his feet. ""I've never been more sure about anything in my life than I am now," she said, kissing him while the room *awwwed*.

When she released him, he took a step back. She saw the pink in his cheeks and the tears shimmering in his eyes as he slid the ring onto her left hand.

"A perfect fit," he said.

"We were, all along," she marveled.

Teo smiled at her and offered his elbow. "We should head downstairs, future Mrs. Abara. Are you ready?"

"Ready."

12

———

As they were announced, Treasure and Teo entered the main ballroom area to flashing cameras, and seemingly all eyes glued to them. They were the last to be seated, and when Treasure took her spot at the head of the table, the doors to the ballroom closed and she was handed a microphone.

"Ladies and gentlemen of Milos, distinguished guests, family, and friends, I'd like to thank you all for converging here for the Shifter Hellenic Island Talks this year."

She allowed a round of applause before broaching the next topic. "I'm sorry to say that my father, King Ambrose, is resting in his quarters this evening after an illness and will not be able to join us."

A hush fell over the crowd, and a few questions were murmured.

"Can you elaborate on the condition of the king?" a voice asked loudly.

"Is he expected to attend the talks?" asked another.

The sound of a chair scraping back preceded the voice of a reporter Treasure recognized. "A contact of mine claims the king was attacked last night. Abducted and experimented on as part of Zagan's plans to steal royal blood. Can you corroborate that these statements are true?"

"My people of Milos..." Treasure held up a hand as the sound of unrest began to grow. "The king is well cared for, and while it's yet unknown if he can attend any of the talks, as he needs his rest, I will assure you that I will be there in his stead. The topic of Zagan and his experimentation is one we're paying careful attention to, and I'd like to reassure you that I have every intention of protecting you all. I'm a highly trained Furry United Coalition Agent who is working closely with our Bonafide Security, so I can assure you that security will be highly present at the talks."

"Can you tell us what else you will cover during the talks?" another reporter asked.

"Actually, yes," Treasure said, smiling brightly at the chance to change the topic. She looked to Teo. "King Mateo, will you do the honors, please?"

Mateo stepped up beside her, taking her hand in his and then holding it up for the crowd to see. "After many years of a postponed betrothal, the Leatherback Princess of Milos, Treasure Garner, and I, King Cock Mateo Abara of the Madagascar rock agama lizards, are officially announcing our engagement."

From that point on, the dinner moved forward without a hitch. The dance after the dinner was full of guests, reporters, and dignitaries approaching the happy couple to congratulate them—only after each of Treasure's sisters had a chance to look at the ring up close, squeal, and give her a hug.

When the festivities finally ended and the ballroom emptied, Treasure and Teo moved to leave, just to be stopped by Harriet and Lear.

"You need to spill! That proposal is totally unexpected! I mean clever when it came to diverting the press, but why didn't either of you say something earlier?" Harriet asked.

"I mean I understand you are betrothed to one another, but is this merely a stunt, or are you really going to make a go of it?" Lear asked.

"How did this even *happen*?" Harriet asked. "Last I heard, Treasure was *never* going to meet her betrothed."

"Guys! Slow down! We will answer all of your questions, I promise!" Treasure said with a giggle. "It turns out that both of our fathers came up with a plan, and Stan over at FUCN'A agreed to help. So we meet each other and ended up at dinner at the Hub, and the rest is history."

"Okay, but I heard there was a whole fight once you got off the jet," Harriet said.

"I was angry when I first found out it had all been a setup. I'd even assumed Teo was in on the whole thing, but love conquers all, and it was too late to turn back. Not once I'd already had the chance to fall for him." Treasure looked up at Teo and smiled.

"Well, then I guess there's only one other question—when's the wedding?"

"Harriet! Slow down! Let me enjoy this moment for a bit. I mean Father doesn't even know yet..." Treasure's voice trailed as she made the statement, and she lowered her head and sighed.

Mateo tightened his grip around her shoulder. "He's going to be okay, Treasure."

"I'd like to go check on him before we retire for the evening."

"Of course."

Harriet and Lear followed them to her father's quarters.

The guards outside his doors looked jubilant, and Teo dared to hope. "Is there a change in the king?"

Without answering, they opened the door, and they all stepped into the room buzzing with excitement. "He's awake!" someone shouted before Treasure and Teo were thrust through the apartment into the king's bedroom.

"Father!" Treasure cried, throwing herself onto his bed and hugging him. "I can't tell you how happy I am that you're awake."

"There, there, my daughter," he said, patting her hair. "I'm fine."

When she finally released him, Teo offered her a chair. "Are you, though?" Treasure asked. "Fine, that is. Are you fine?"

King Ambrose nodded, taking Treasure's hand in his. "After Zagan stuck me, I wasn't able to move or shift. They tell me it was similar to what he's used before, but now it's more long-lasting."

"Yes, that's what they'd been saying," Treasure replied.

"We will need to triple security for tomorrow. I want everyone to feel safe," the king said before his gaze fell on Treasure's hand and then flicked up to Teo. "Am I gaining a son?"

"Oh! Father, it's, well—" Treasure's voice trailed.

"Yes, Your Highness," Teo said.

"Well, this is splendid news indeed! When I am more like myself, we will have the grandest of parties to celebrate this engagement."

Treasure offered him a small smile. "I think that sounds lovely, Father."

"Does this mean I'm forgiven for my subterfuge?"

"Yes, of course." Treasure gave him a kiss on his cheek before her brows furrowed. "Are you feeling well enough to go to the talks?"

He squeezed her hand. "Darling, I think it's about time that this old man tries on retirement. Given what has been reported to me about how you handled tonight, I am certain the people of Milos are in good hands."

"Father, what are you talking about? I can't just lead the kingdom right now."

"Well, you officially can't until we have the coronation ceremony, but I think you can take my place for now while I take some much-deserved rest. You'll do lovely at the talks. I have faith you'll run SHIT right. Now, you two get some rest. You have a big day tomorrow. And congratulations. I knew all along that Teo was your rock. I'm just glad that now you know it too."

Treasure kissed her father's forehead, and Teo followed her out of her father's apartment. As they walked the hallway to her room, she stopped at a portrait of her father.

"It's hard to imagine seeing a painting of my likeness up there next to my father," she said as she let out a long breath.

"I'm sure it will look just as stunning as you, Treasure." Teo kissed her temple.

"He said I'm doing well. I think that's the first time he ever uttered those words without following it with some form of criticism. It's strange and a little hard to process. I guess he now sees me as an adult and not his little girl. But queen? It's a big responsibility."

Teo palmed her shoulders and met her eyes. "It's a responsibility that you will handle with grace because you've got your rock right here."

She drew him into her arms and kissed his cheek. "I was hoping you'd say that. Together, forever."

"Together forever and always."

13

The sun peeked out over the horizon and lit up Treasure's bedroom, gently waking her.

She rose from her bed and stretched. Despite her fear, she actually slept well, and she attributed that partly to the fact that her father had recovered and partly to the fact that she'd had a god sleeping next to her.

Teo's face looked so peaceful that she didn't want to wake him, but they had a busy day ahead. She was about to give him a nudge when he started to stir on his own.

"I'm definitely enjoying this," he said as he stretched his arms into the air.

"What do you mean?"

"I rather enjoy waking up to such a pretty face

every morning." He cupped her cheek and drew her lips to his. "And I declare that our morning routine should always include a kiss."

Treasure smiled. "I second that declaration. Come on, let's get a shower in. We have a lot to do before the talks."

"It's going to be torture to shower with you without being able to make love to you. You know that, right?"

"It will be hard, yes, but I'm certain we can handle it. Not to mention all the water we will be conserving by taking one together."

"You've got me there."

The two readied themselves for the day, and when they emerged from the bedroom, they found a breakfast spread waiting in Treasure's sitting room.

"I'm positive we are ready for the security aspect of the talks, but how are you feeling about speaking in front of your people, Treasure?" Teo asked after pouring them each a cup of coffee.

"It is still a shock that my father wants to retire. I really thought that I'd never see the day. But, if last night is any indication of what is to come, I'm sure I can handle today."

"That's good to hear."

The two finished breakfast and headed to the

convention area, walking past the stage and seating and inspecting all the grounds. While they did, they checked in with different agents, ensuring there had been no sign of Zagan or any of his cronies.

Then they took their place at the welcome entrance to greet everyone as they entered.

Finally, once all were seated, Treasure took her place at the podium.

"Ladies and gentlemen, I am princess Treasure Gardner of Milos, and I'd like to welcome you all to the annual Shifter Hellenic Island Talks. This year we will be discussing the prevention of the capture of shifters through nets from fishing boats on the sea and poaching around the world. I would like to officially open up the talks now."

As she started to step aside for the first speaker, an all too familiar figure flew in from above them—a winged bull. And then a number of guards, along with a half-shifted Lear and Harriet—a leatherback and a hare—came rushing to the platform.

"Treasure! Look out! It's Zagan!" Teo shouted.

Before Teo could reach her and before Treasure could shift into her leatherback turtle, Zagan injected a vial into her upper arm.

"Treasure!" Teo screamed as he turned into his phoenix-rock agama hybrid.

It was the first time she saw him in his magnificent glory. His wings spanned a good twenty feet and were a gorgeous regal blue with fiery red and gold tips. His head had scales and was also a fiery red. His lizard body and long tail were a regal blue with flecks and stripes of sky blue that looked almost as if they were hand-painted on his body. She basked in the glory of him until everything went black.

He couldn't lose her, not after getting her back. Anger welled in his gut as Zagan flew off with Treasure's now lifeless body, and then a pang of fear crept up Teo's spine.

What did he do to her?

His rock phoenix had instantly come to the forefront as Zagan began to fly up into the sky above them. Teo leaped into the air, fast on Zagan's tail.

"Let her go!" he commanded, having enough control of his shift to keep his human features— including face, mouth, and vocal cords.

Zagan only screeched as he continued to gain altitude.

Teo's body radiated flames in hues of red, orange, yellow, and blue as he followed the shifter into the air. He flung his long tail up toward Zagan, spearing the bull-bird hybrid.

It worked. Zagan hadn't expected the blow, and the impact caused him to drop Treasure.

Teo was ready. He coiled his tail around her and tucked her into one of his large wings while flames continued to surge around his body. He gathered energy within him, transforming his human facial features into his lizard face, then shot flames through his snout toward Zagan.

The hot blue flames encircled Zagan's wings. The shifter let out a blood-curdling scream as he became unable to maintain his flight and plummeted into the Aegean Sea.

Teo hovered and waited a few moments to gauge if Zagan would surface.

Around him, Harriet and Lear's drones and some other aerial shifters gathered, some starting to circle the area.

Satisfied it was taken care of, Teo descended from the sky, gently laying Treasure down onto the beautiful Milos beach.

I can't lose you, Treasure, he thought.

He embraced the painful idea of living a long life without her, giving himself to the grief.

He sailed away on the emotion until a single

phoenix tear welled up in his eye.

He leaned over her, dropping the tear onto her, praying that the myth of the magical properties was true.

Within seconds, an aura of red light surrounded Treasure's entire body, and she stirred.

Then opened her eyes.

"Teo?" She reached for him, and he quickly shifted back to human form.

"I'm here, Treasure."

Treasure blinked then seemed to remember what had happened. She sat up, looking around. "Where's Zagan?"

"He's gone."

Treasure pawed at Teo's chest, trying to gain balance to stand up.

"No way. You rest for a minute." His words purred in her ear.

"How long was I out? Why am I here on the beach and not in bed, like Father was when he woke up?"

"You weren't out long at all. Apparently, your guy has the magic touch. His phoenix tears woke you." Teo looked up to see Lear and Harriet standing nearby. He hadn't even noticed them approach.

Treasure searched Teo's eyes for an answer. He

sighed, relieved that she was okay finally hitting him. "I didn't know if it would work, but I had to try."

She smiled then wrapped her arms around him. "Well, I guess I'm lucky to have a healing rock by my side."

"The thought of losing you, Treasure... I don't know what I would have done if..." Teo's voice trailed.

"You can't get rid of me that easily!" Treasure said as she cupped his face. "Together forever."

"And always." Teo palmed her hand on his cheek before continuing, "Are you feeling well enough to speak, or do you want me to address everyone?"

"I will speak."

Teo helped her up, and they walked from the beach back to the convention area. She approached the podium, standing tall and proud. She lowered the microphone before addressing the crowd.

"My people of Milos, Zagan may have been dealt with, but we are still vulnerable to attacks like this one today. Now more than ever we must put aside our differences and fight our common enemies. There will always be another Zagan, so from this day forward, I propose that we all protect ourselves by protecting others around us. United, we can defeat this band of perpetrators hell-bent on stealing our blood."

A roar of cheers from the crowd emerged, and Treasure raised a hand to silence them so she could continue speaking. "It is Milos's tradition to go on with the talks to show our enemies that we do not fear them."

"Yes, it is, but I think it's time we break from that tradition," a voice said from behind Treasure.

She turned toward the voice, and her father came into her sight. "Father?"

Her eyes searched his. "Who's up for a little celebration?" King Ambrose asked the crowd.

Another cheer roared through the crowd. "Very well! Follow me to the ballroom where I've planned a glorious banquet to celebrate my daughter's engagement!"

"Is this why you didn't want to speak at the talks? You were planning a banquet?" Treasure asked her father in a hushed tone.

"Perhaps," King Ambrose said with a smile as he pulled Treasure into his arms.

He then looked over at Mateo.

"Take good care of her. She's precious."

"Always, Your Majesty. Always."

The End.

Not quite! There are more FUC Academy books coming soon!

To find out more about these books and more, visit worlds.EveLanglais.com or sign up for the EveL Worlds newsletter. If you haven't already downloaded the **free Academy intro** (written by Eve Langlais) make sure you grab it on our website!

The Turtle and the Hare

What happens when pure hare-itage meets royal blood?

When Prince Lear comes face to face with Harriet, he's smitten. Fast of word and fleet of foot, not only is this hare his lucky charm, she's his mate too.

As if his royal turtleness didn't have enough to balance on his back, a plot is afoot to steal his royal blood. Can Harriet keep him safe?

The Ferret and the Fossa

This ferret is about to tunnel her way into this fossa's heart!

When the fantastically fragrant ferret moves in and takes over the fossa's space, will he remain a creature of habit? Or will these two unlikely allies bond while discovering the truth about Rayan's father?

The Lynx and the Llama

This lynx doesn't want any drama, but the new llama in town is making her purr.

Erika Jean's life had been turned to shambles by her ex, but ever since working for King Rayan, things have been looking up. Until she's asked to go undercover... in a fake relationship!

The Lamb and the Llama

She'll find love when lambs fly.

With Zagan escaped from prison, Amira and Richard find themselves in uncharted territory. Can they capture the bad guy and navigate their curious feelings toward each other without breaking too many rules?

ABOUT THE AUTHOR

USA Today best-selling and award-winning author Amanda Kimberley has written in various genres in the course of almost four decades.

Her nonfiction blog, which focuses on the chronic disease fibromyalgia has garnered recognition from various organizations, including *Health Magazine*, naming her blog, *Fibro and Fabulous*, as a top blog for fibro sufferers. Amanda has also written for medical magazines and sites like FM Aware, The National Fibromyalgia Association's magazine, and ProHealth.

When Kimberley is not writing nonfiction, she enjoys penning romance. Her first Furry United Coalition story, *The Turtle and the Hare*, earned the 2020 Summer Splash Book Awards of Ink and Scratches for Best Romance. Her Forever Series Books, Forever Friends and Forever Bound, were featured in 2015 and 2016 on the BookCountry website, a division of Penguin/Random House, as editor's picks. She has also been featured as a *USA Today* Happy Ever After Hot List Indie Author with *Claiming My Valentine*, a Best Poet of the '90s ranking for an anthology, and she has had a #1 PNR ranking with *Immortal Hunger* and *Hearts Unleashed*.

Amanda Kimberley is a Connecticut native that now lives in the warmth of Northern Texas with her zoo, which consists of her husky tuxedo cat, hamsters, rabbits, guinea pigs, a tank of fish, two daughters, and a husband. When she is not writing, you can find her cooking whole foods for her pack. She also enjoys reading, hiking, and gaming.

Find her online:

- Website: authoramandakimberley.com

- BookBub: bookbub.com/profile/amanda-kimberley
- Facebook Group: facebook.com/groups/AmandaKimberleysReaderGroup

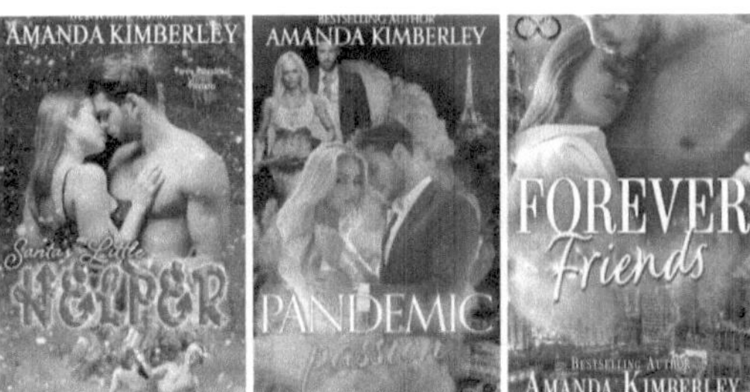